#16: Alien Androids Assault Arizona

Johnathan Rand

An AudioCraft Publishing, Inc. book

This book is a work of fiction. Names, places, characters and incidents are used fictitiously, or are products of the author's very active imagination.

Graphics layout/design consultant: Scott Beard, Straits Area Printing
Honorary graphics consultant: Chuck Beard *(we miss you, Chuck)*
Editors: Cindee Rocheleau, Sheri Kelley

Book warehouse and storage facilities provided by Clarence and Dorienne's Storage, Car Rental & Shuttle Service, Topinabee Island, MI

Warehouse security provided by Salty, Abby and Lily Munster.

American Chillers #16: Alien Androids Assault Arizona
Paperback edition ISBN 1-893699-69-2
Hardcover edition ISBN 1-893699-70-6

ALIEN
ANDROIDS
ASSAULT
ARIZONA

VISIT CHILLERMANIA!

WORLD HEADQUARTERS FOR BOOKS BY JOHNATHAN RAND!

CHILLERMANIA!

**I-75 Exit 313
then south
1 mile!**

Visit the HOME for books by Johnathan Rand! Featuring books, hats, shirts, bookmarks and other cool stuff not available anywhere else in the world! Plus, watch the American Chillers website for news of special events and signings at *CHILLERMANIA!* with author Johnathan Rand! Located in northern lower Michigan, on I-75! Take exit 313 . . . then south 1 mile! For more info, call (231) 238-0338. And be afraid! Be veeeery afraaaaaaiiiid . . . .

1

"Arielle!" I shouted, waving my hand in the air. "Over here!"

From across the lunchroom, Arielle Watkins saw me and started walking toward the table I was sitting at. Arielle moved here last year, and we've become pretty good friends. She's tall for her age, with long, dark brown hair.

Directly across from me sat Joey Romaniello. Joey lives on the same block that I do, and I've known him ever since he moved to Scottsdale a couple of years ago. He said that he used to live in Minnesota, but he likes Arizona better because it's warmer, and we don't get any snow.

And he's sure right about that! Scottsdale can get pretty hot in the summertime, that's for sure.

"Hi Shelby," Arielle said to me. "Did you get your math homework done?" She sat down next to me and placed her sack lunch on the table.

"Yeah," I replied, taking a bite of my sandwich.

"That was the hardest homework assignment I think I've ever had!" she said. "I never thought fifth grade math would be so difficult. I just know that I'm going to get most of the answers wrong."

"I didn't think it was that hard," Joey said. "I finished it last night and still had time to go to the arcade before it got dark."

"Yeah, but you're good at math," I said. "I thought that the problems were pretty hard. Sometimes Mrs. Rodriguez gives us way too much homework. Every time she gives us a homework assignment, I'm terrified."

"You've got that right," Arielle said.

Joey finished chewing his sandwich. He dug into his pocket and pulled out a small, gold-colored pendant. It was about the size of a quarter.

"What's that?" I asked.

"Oh, I won it last night at the arcade. At first, I thought it was gold . . . but it's only cheap plastic."

He flipped the pendant into the air and it fell onto the table. I snapped it up and looked at it.

"Yeah, it would be cool if it was real gold," I said. "But it's still kind of neat looking."

"You can have it if you want," Joey said, unwrapping a candy bar.

"Really?" I said.

"Yeah," he replied.

"It would make a cool necklace," I said. "I'll make a necklace out of it, and it can be my good luck charm."

And when I went home from school, that's exactly what I did. I have a thin gold chain that I got for my birthday last year, and I looped it through the pendant. Then I put the necklace on.

It actually looked pretty cool. I know that the pendant was only cheap plastic, but from a few feet away, it looked real.

"There," I said aloud as I looked into the mirror. "Now I have my good luck charm. I wonder what kind of good luck it will bring me."

As it turned out, I was going to need all of the good luck I could get . . . because the very next day, I was going to find out something horrifying about my very own teacher, Mrs. Rodriguez.

And it would have nothing to do with homework!

2

Wednesday started off normal. I got up, dressed, ate a bowl of cereal, and walked to school. Same old routine that I do every weekday. I ate lunch in the cafeteria with Joey and Arielle . . . just like always.

And when the bell rang and it was time to go home, I stuffed all my books into my backpack and left the classroom.

Joey stopped me in the hall.

"Do you want to go for a bike ride later?" he asked.

"I would, but I'm supposed to go with my mom and dad to some dinner. Dad's on a bowling league, and tonight is some kind of awards banquet."

"*That* sounds like fun," Joey smirked, rolling his eyes.

I shook my head. "Yeah, it'll probably be pretty boring. Maybe we'll go for a bike ride tomorrow."

"Sure," Joey said, and he walked off.

15

I turned and began walking down the hall. Then I suddenly realized that I had left my favorite pen on my desk.

I turned around and headed back to the classroom, waving goodbye to some of my classmates. When I got back to Mrs. Rodriguez's room, I stopped at the door.

And stared.

Mrs. Rodriguez had her back to me. She was the only one in the room, and she was staring straight at the wall . . . *talking into her watch!*

But there was more to it than that. Sure, talking into a watch was strange, but it was how she was speaking that was really weird.

Mrs. Rodriguez sounded like a robot!

Her voice was mechanical and very monotone, and she didn't sound at all like she normally sounded. From where I stood in the hall, I couldn't quite make out what she was saying. She sure sounded odd, though, and I wasn't going to interrupt her. I could see my pen on my desk, and I decided that I would just leave it until tomorrow.

Without warning, Mrs. Rodriguez turned and looked at me. She lowered her wrist and stopped speaking. Her eyes had a glazed, cold look. She looked creepy.

And suddenly, she smiled.

"Hello Shelby," she said sweetly, in a perfectly normal voice. "Can I help you?"

"Uh, um," I stammered. "I, uh . . . I forgot my pen."

She looked at my desk, then walked to it and picked up my pen. "This one?" she asked.

16

I nodded, and Mrs. Rodriguez brought the pen to me. "Here you are, dear," she said. "And don't forget that your book report is due tomorrow."

"Yeah," I replied, taking the pen from her. "I'm almost finished."

"Good. I'll see you in class tomorrow."

"See you," I said, and I turned and walked down the hall.

That was weird. I mean . . . Mrs. Rodriguez has always been very nice, but I've never seen her talking into her watch before.

When I got outside, I saw Arielle on the playground. She was talking to some friends. When she saw me, she left the group and walked up to me.

"I thought you'd be gone by now," she said.

I held up my pen. "I forgot this," I said. "Say . . . have you ever seen Mrs. Rodriguez acting weird?"

"What do you mean by 'weird'?" she asked.

"Oh, I don't know. Like . . . speaking in a strange voice?"

"You mean a different language? Sure. She speaks Spanish, and I think—"

"No, not another language," I said. "Just . . . in a weird voice. And talking into her watch."

Arielle gave me her own weird look. "Talking into her watch? I think you've been watching too much television."

"I'm serious!" I said. "I just saw her talking into her watch. She sounded like a robot."

"You're imagining things," Arielle replied. "There's nothing wrong with Mrs. Rodriguez."

Maybe Arielle was right. Maybe I just *imagined* that I heard my teacher acting strange.

But I didn't think so. I *know* what I saw. I *know* what I *heard.*

"Well, I've got to go," Arielle said. "I have to finish my book report."

"Yeah, me, too," I replied. "See you tomorrow."

And as she walked off, I hoped that she didn't think I was acting silly. Maybe I shouldn't have said anything about Mrs. Rodriguez.

But the very next day, Arielle came running up to me at lunchtime. The cafeteria was packed, and she hustled up to the table where Joey and I were sitting.

"Shelby!" Arielle whispered loudly. Her eyes were wide with excitement. *"You're right! I just came from Mrs. Rodriguez's room . . . and you won't believe what I saw!"*

3

Arielle sat next to me.

"What?!?!" I exclaimed. "What did you see?!?!"

"Well, I was walking by our classroom," Arielle replied, "and when I looked inside, Mrs. Rodriguez . . . was eating a sandwich! It was horrifying!" Arielle placed her hands to her cheeks and gasped like she was scared out of her wits.

She was making fun of me!

Joey started to laugh, and then Arielle started laughing, too.

"Funny," I snapped. "Real funny."

"Come on," Arielle said as she opened her lunch bag. "I was only kidding."

"I'm telling you Mrs. Rodriguez was acting strange," I said.

"So?" Arielle said. She pulled out a wrapped sandwich and placed it on the table. "Lots of people act strange. You can't go to jail for acting weird."

She had a point. But I was still convinced that something funny was going on.

I just didn't know what.

"Did you get your book report finished?" Joey asked.

"Yeah," I said, taking a bite of my sandwich. "I finished it last night."

"What book did you read, Shelby?" Arielle asked. She had unwrapped her sandwich, and after she spoke she took a bite.

"The Incredible Journey," I replied. "It was really good."

Joey looked at my neck. "Hey," he said. "You really *did* make a necklace out of that thing."

I reached up and held the small plastic pendant between my fingers. "Yeah. If you're not real close, it looks like real gold. It's my new good luck charm."

"Has it brought you any good luck?" Arielle asked.

"Not yet," I replied.

"I read *Hatchet,*" Joey said, returning the subject of discussion to our book reports. "It was really good, too."

"I'm going to write my own story," I said. "It's going to be about a teacher that isn't really a teacher, but a robot."

Arielle laughed. "Do you still think that Mrs. Rodriguez is up to something strange?" she asked.

"I don't know," I said, taking another bite of my sandwich. "But I know what I saw and heard yesterday."

"She seemed pretty normal this morning," Joey said.

"You guys can say what you want," I said, after I gulped down another bite. "But she was acting weird yesterday. I guess it doesn't mean anything, but I'm going to be watching to see if she does it again."

We finished our lunches and trudged back to the classroom. Mrs. Rodriguez was already at her desk, going over our book reports.

And the rest of the afternoon we did the same things we usually do. We read silently for a while, then we studied state history, which was actually kind of fun. I found out a lot about Arizona that I hadn't known. Arizona is famous for the Grand Canyon, which most people know. But I didn't know that the word 'Arizona' is from the Aztec Indian word *arizuma*. It means 'silver-bearing'.

The bell rang, and it was time to go home. I got up to leave.

"Shelby?" Mrs. Rodriguez said.

I turned.

"Yes?" I replied.

"May I see you for a moment after class?"

Gulp.

"Um . . . okay," I said. My classmates had started to file out of the room. Soon, everyone was gone.

Mrs. Rodriguez looked at me sternly. "This matter is very important," she said.

My mouth suddenly went dry, and I swallowed hard. Whatever was going to happen next, I knew that it wasn't going to be good.

4

"Really, Mrs. Rodriguez," I suddenly blurted out. "I won't tell anyone that you're a robot! Really I won't!"

Suddenly, Mrs. Rodriguez smiled. "Oh Shelby," she said with a chuckle. "Don't be silly. I'm not a robot."

Relief fell over me like a bucket of water.

"I did want to see you, though," she said. She turned to her desk and picked up a paper. "This is yours."

She handed the paper to me. It was my book report. At the top was an A+.

"Congratulations," she said. "That is one of the finest book reports I have ever read. You should be very proud."

I couldn't believe it! I had never received an A+ for anything in my life!

Mrs. Rodriguez spent a few minutes explaining why she thought my report was so good. I was really glad, of course, because I'd worked hard on it. But I didn't expect to get an A+!

Then Mrs. Rodriguez changed the subject.

"There are a few rumors going around that I am a robot," she said. "Have you heard them?"

"Uh . . . um," I stuttered. "Uh . . . yeah."

"Do you know how they may have started?" she asked. Her blue eyes had gone cold, and a chill swept over me.

"Well, uh, no," I replied.

"Do you think I'm a robot?" she asked icily. Her eyes never left mine.

"Um . . . no, I, I guess not."

"You *guess* not?" she replied.

"I mean . . . I mean, no, you're not," I said.

And suddenly I felt very silly. Here I was, still afraid that my own teacher might be a robot. It was ridiculous, and I felt very foolish.

"Then it's settled. Run along, and I'll see you tomorrow. And congratulations again on an excellent book report!"

"Thank you, Mrs. Rodriguez," I said. I turned and walked out of the room.

When I reached the main doors, I felt foolish for the second time that day. In my rush to leave the classroom, I had left my book report on my desk! Mom and Dad would want to see it for sure, especially since I got an A+.

I turned around and hurried back to Mrs. Rodriguez's class . . . but before I went in, I heard a strange voice.

It was the same voice I'd heard the day before!

24

I slowly stretched out my neck and stuck my head into the door, just far enough to see.

What I saw was scary . . . and the words I heard were chilling.

"No, she doesn't suspect anything," Mrs. Rodriguez was saying in that weird, robotic voice. *"I talked to her about it, and she doesn't suspect a thing anymore."*

I was *right!* Mrs. Rodriguez was a robot!

But what's so bad about a robot teacher?

Lots . . . as I was about to find out.

5

As you can imagine, I was freaked out. I turned and ran down the hall and outside, forgetting all about my book report. When I remembered it on the way home, there was no way that I was going to go back for it.

But what would I do in the morning? I would have to face Mrs. Rodriguez again . . . only now, I was sure that she was some sort of robot.

And that night, I had some really horrible nightmares. I dreamed that Mrs. Rodriguez was a robot and she malfunctioned, giving everyone in the class weeks and weeks worth of homework.

Now, that might not be scary to *you*, but it sure was to *me*.

In another dream, Mrs. Rodriguez was chasing after me. There were wires coming out of her ears, and electricity shot from her fingers. It was such a bad nightmare that it woke me up.

The next morning, I was terrified to go to school. I told my mom that I was sick and should stay home, but she said that I looked fine and that I wasn't running a temperature, and that I'd have to go.

Rats.

As soon as I got to school, I searched until I found Joey. He was standing with some of his friends near the cafeteria. When he saw me, I waved him over.

"What's up?" he asked.

"Everything!" I exclaimed. "I was right! Mrs. Rodriguez is a robot!"

"Get real!" he said, shaking his head. "You tried that on me yesterday!"

"She really is!" I insisted.

Just then, Arielle walked up to us. Her backpack was slung over her shoulder, and she let it slip to the floor.

"Shelby is back on her robot kick," Joey smirked.

"Oh yeah?" Arielle said with a sly smile.

"I'm really serious you guys," I said. "I saw her again last night. After school. She was talking in that same voice that I told you about before. Only now, she was talking to someone about *me!*"

"About *you?!?!*" Arielle said. "Now I've heard everything!"

"She was!" I exclaimed. "She didn't know I was listening. She was talking into her watch, telling someone

28

how I didn't suspect anything anymore. I'm telling you . . . there's something going on!"

"Well, let's go ask her," Joey said.

"Are you kidding?!?!" I replied. "She'll deny it. She doesn't want anyone to know she's a robot!"

"You seem to know a lot about something you don't know much about," Arielle said.

"I know one thing for sure: our teacher is a robot, and that's a fact."

"All right," Joey said. "Let's go to class. She's probably there right now."

"No!" I said.

"Why not?" Arielle asked. "I mean . . . she's been here for a few years and she's never hurt anyone. What do we have to worry about?"

She had a point. Even if Mrs. Rodriguez *did* turn out to be a robot, she hasn't ever hurt anyone.

And so, the three of us decided to go to class early. I would ask Mrs. Rodriguez about her strange behavior. Maybe there really *was* a logical explanation as to what was going on.

And besides . . . it was the right thing to do. If Mrs. Rodriguez *wasn't* a robot, it wouldn't be fair to say things about her behind her back.

"You're wrong, you know," Joey said as we made our way toward the classroom. "Mrs. Rodriguez isn't a robot."

In a way, he was right.

Mrs. Rodriguez *wasn't* a robot.

But she wasn't human, either.

She was worse—a lot worse . . . and that's where my life changed. I was about to know horror . . . real, deep, tangible horror . . . like I had never known before in my life.

6

I have to admit I was really nervous as the three of us walked down the hall to our classroom. School didn't actually begin for another ten minutes, but there were kids in the hall, chatting and laughing, putting things in and taking things out of their lockers. A couple of students were sitting on the floor, reading. Others were gathered in small groups, talking, waiting for school to start.

And up ahead, I could see the door of our classroom. It was open, and the light was on.

I stopped in the hall. Arielle and Joey stopped and turned.

"What's the matter?" Arielle asked.

"I'm just not sure about this," I said. "Maybe this isn't a good idea. Maybe Mrs. Rodriguez will get mad."

"But you said she's a robot," Joey said. "Why are you worried if she gets mad?"

"Because . . . well, just in case I'm wrong," I said. "I don't want her mad at me. And I don't want to hurt her feelings, either."

"Oh, come on," Arielle said. "She'll probably think that it's funny."

My feet began to move, but it was a funny feeling. It was like they moved on their own, as if they had their own mind.

The three of us continued down the hall. Two kids ran by us, and we had to dart out of their way to avoid getting bumped into.

Suddenly, we found ourselves at the door of our classroom. I peered inside. Mrs. Rodriguez was at her desk. She was wearing her glasses, examining some papers. When she saw us, she looked up.

"Why, hello Shelby. Good morning Arielle and Joey."

"Hi," the three of us said in unison.

"Class doesn't begin for another ten minutes," Mrs. Rodriguez said. She reached up and removed her glasses. "Is there something I can help you with?"

"Well, I, um . . . ." I stammered. I felt silly, but, then again, I couldn't forget the strange sight in this very classroom yesterday afternoon, when I'd spotted Mrs. Rodriguez talking into her watch. I just knew that she was talking about me.

Joey spoke up. "What she's trying to say," he said to Mrs. Rodriguez, "is that she thinks you're a robot."

"Why Shelby," Mrs. Rodriguez said. She stood up and walked toward the three of us standing in the doorway.

Behind us, the flurry of activity continued as students readied for the school day. "We discussed this yesterday. Why is it that you *still* think such a silly thing?" She walked up to us and stopped, placing her hands on her hips. She didn't look mad or anything, but there was something in her glare that made me feel uneasy. Nervous.

"I . . . I don't know for sure," I said sheepishly. "But I saw you talking into your watch yesterday. You were talking about me. You were telling someone that I didn't suspect anything."

Her eyes never left mine. Not once did Mrs. Rodriguez look at Arielle or Joey. It was kind of eerie.

Then she smiled, but it didn't look like a happy smile. It looked phony, like she was doing her best to smile, even though she didn't mean it. Like she was acting. She slipped the watch off her wrist and held it out to me.

"Go ahead," she said. "Look at it. It's just a normal watch. I don't talk to it."

I took the watch and inspected it. Although I wasn't familiar with the brand, it didn't look like any sort of radio or communication device. After a moment, I handed it back to her.

"Shelby, you have a very good imagination. Sometimes I talk to myself. Have you ever done that?"

I nodded, and so did Arielle and Joey.

"Well, maybe you heard me talking to myself," she said. "Maybe you only *thought* that I was talking about you."

"That's probably it," Arielle said.

Then Mrs. Rodriguez laughed. "I promise you, Shelby, that I'm *not* a robot." She laughed again, just as the morning bell rang. "Come in," she said. "We have a busy day today." She turned and walked back to her desk.

"See?" Joey said. "She's not a robot. It was probably just your imagination."

Students began pushing their way around us to get into class, and I walked across the room and took my seat. Joey sat at his desk on the other side of the room, and Arielle sat two desks behind me. Mrs. Rodriguez took attendance, and the school day started.

But all day, I kept a careful watch on Mrs. Rodriguez. I caught her looking at me more than she normally does. When she saw me watching her she looked away, like she'd been caught.

And by the end of the day, I knew that something was going on. Maybe Arielle and Joey didn't believe me, but I *knew* that Mrs. Rodriguez was hiding something. I didn't know what it was, but I had a perfect plan to find out for sure.

I was going to follow Mrs. Rodriguez home. She doesn't live far, and she walks to school in the morning, and walks home in the afternoon. I would follow her home, and prove once and for all that she was a robot.

7

After school, I told Joey and Arielle that I was going to take the long way back to my house. Which was true, because if I followed Mrs. Rodriguez to her home, I would have to walk several more blocks before I made it back to my house.

I waited on the playground until I saw Mrs. Rodriguez come out. Then, as she left the school grounds and crossed a street, I began following her from a distance, ducking behind trees now and then to make sure she wouldn't see me. She never looked back, though, and soon, she was walking up the driveway to her house. I watched her reach into her purse and pull out her house key, slide it into the lock, and open the door. Then she was inside.

I felt odd spying on her. It's not a nice thing to do, and I wouldn't ever do it if I wasn't one hundred percent sure I was right.

Spying on a human being might be wrong, but spying on a robot? I was sure that was all right.

Quickly, I darted across the street and behind a row of bushes that were near her house. I was hoping that I could get close enough to hear her talking, if she was speaking to anyone. And I was on the lookout for anything strange, too. Like maybe if she plugged herself into the wall to recharge her batteries or something. I know it sounds silly, but I didn't know what to expect from a robot.

I waited in the bushes for a long time, but I didn't see or hear anything. I would have to get closer.

But how? I certainly didn't want to get discovered and get into trouble. On the other hand, my curiosity was getting the best of me. I just had to know the truth.

Ducking down, I left my hiding place in the bushes and scurried up to Mrs. Rodriguez's house. From here, I could creep along below the window without her seeing me. The living room window was open, and I thought that if I crept under it, I would be able to hear her if she was talking to another robot or something.

On my hands and knees, I crept along the side of the house until I reached the porch. Above me, the living room window was open. I could hear Mrs. Rodriguez saying something, but her voice was muffled and distant.

Suddenly, her voice grew nearer. Before I knew what was happening, the front door was open, and Mrs. Rodriguez was standing above me, holding a telephone to her ear, glaring down at me.

I'd been caught!

8

I knew right then and there that I was in a lot of trouble. Not necessarily because I had been spying on my teacher, but because I just *knew* that she was a robot.

And she knew that I knew.

"Shelby Crusado," she said sternly. Then she spoke into the phone. "Thank you, Mary Kay. I've found her." She pressed a button on the phone and terminated the connection, then spoke to me. "Just what are you doing here, young lady?"

I didn't know what to say. I didn't want to come right out and say that I was spying on her, but that's what I was doing.

And so, I didn't say anything. Besides . . . I was terrified. I don't think I could have said anything if I had wanted to. My stomach felt like a cement ball was bouncing around inside. Fear ate at my temples. I really *was* scared.

And Mrs. Rodriguez knew it, too. She sat down on the porch steps. "Come here Shelby. Sit down."

I did as she asked, sitting on the porch steps. But not too close.

"Mrs. Marsh across the street phoned me to tell me that a prowler was in the bushes near my house. I had a feeling it might be you. You still think that I'm not human, don't you?"

I nodded, and Mrs. Rodriguez laughed. "Oh, Shelby," she said. "You and your imagination. Have you ever thought about becoming an author? You have some very interesting ideas in that head of yours."

Still, I couldn't help but think that behind her eyes wasn't a human at all, but something electronic. Something man-made. Even though she was smiling and laughing, there was something very cold about her.

Like a robot.

"I . . . I don't know what to think," I said. "I saw you acting really strange a couple of times."

"And so you think that I'm a robot because of that? Really, Shelby. I know that you're thinking that I'm hiding something from you. But it's just not the case. Now . . . I'd like you to stop this silliness and go home. I'm sure you have homework to do."

I stood up and walked down the steps, then I turned and looked at Mrs. Rodriguez.

Could I be wrong? I wondered. *Am I really just imagining that Mrs. Rodriguez is something other than a human being?*

"I'll see you in class tomorrow, Shelby," she said as she stood up. "And I promise you . . . I'm not an android." With that, she turned and walked into her house, and I began walking down the driveway.

Suddenly, a chill went down my spine. Then it went back up. I could feel the hairs on the back of my neck begin to rise.

Android? I thought. *I never used the word 'android'. I used the word 'robot'. Why would Mrs. Rodriguez use the word 'android'?*

Simple. She was hiding something. I was getting close to the truth, and Mrs. Rodriguez knew it. She knew it . . . and she didn't like it.

I walked on, and the more I thought about it, the more I just *knew* that I had to get to the bottom of this. I had to find out once and for all.

So I turned around. I started walking back to Mrs. Rodriguez's home, determined to find the truth.

Have you ever wanted something really bad, only to get it and find out that it wasn't what you expected? Well, that's what was about to happen to me.

Not only did I find out some things that I had never expected, I found out things that could only be described as one hundred percent *terrifying*.

9

I kept thinking about that word.

Android.

I had never used that word. Why had Mrs. Rodriguez? Is that what she was? An android?

True, androids and robots were almost the same thing. Androids, however, are built to resemble humans. I've seen a few science fiction television shows with androids, and I've always been fascinated by them.

And I was curious. I was curious, but instead of sneaking around this time, I was going to confront Mrs. Rodriguez and get right to the point. I wasn't going to ask her if she was a robot . . . I was going to ask her if she was an *android.* I would march right up to her front door and ring the doorbell. I knew that I would probably be late for supper, but I didn't care.

I reached up and fingered the ring—my good luck charm—dangling from the thin gold chain around my neck.

Still there.

I returned to Mrs. Rodriguez's house, marched up the driveway, and up to the porch. Confidently, I raised my hand to ring the doorbell . . . but I stopped.

Through the open window, I could hear Mrs. Rodriguez speaking. But her voice wasn't anything like she normally sounded like. Now her voice was oddly mechanical and monotone.

"Yes," she was saying. "I've sent the human away. She had suspected something, but I've taken care of her. She suspects nothing."

I gasped, and my hand flew to my mouth. *I was right all along!*

As I listened, I could hear Mrs. Rodriguez—or whoever she was—speaking. I assumed that she was speaking into a telephone or a radio of some sort, because I couldn't hear the other person that she was talking to. And I didn't dare peek around to look into the window, because she might spot me. I was taking a big risk as it was, standing on the porch in plain sight. But I just had to know more.

"Of course," Mrs. Rodriguez continued in the same odd, mechanical voice. "The plans are underway. It won't be long now."

There was a pause.

"No," Mrs. Rodriguez continued. "The master plans are safe. They are in an ordinary toolbox in the garage, hidden in plain sight. There is no danger of anyone finding them.

When you are ready, I will share the master plans with the others."

Master plans? I thought. *What's being planned? What's going on?*

Well, there was only one way to find out. Mrs. Rodriguez had just said that the master plans—whatever they were—were in the toolbox in her garage.

I took a step back and peered around the house.

The garage door was open. It was open, and I already knew what I was going to do.

I was going to find that toolbox. I was going to find it, and I was going to find the master plan.

10

I dropped to my hands and knees and crawled off the porch, sliding up next to the house. From there, I crawled beneath the windows toward the garage. I could no longer hear Mrs. Rodriguez talking.

Master plans? I kept wondering. *Just what is she talking about?*

I crawled around several bushes, all the while looking around to make sure that no one was watching. I waited for a few moments, and then stood up and sprinted across the driveway and into the darkened garage. There wasn't a car in the garage, so I ducked into a shadowy corner and knelt down, peering out into the street and the houses on the other side. There was no movement. I didn't think anyone was watching.

Toolbox, I thought. *Mrs. Rodriguez said that the master plans were in the tool box.*

I looked around. At the back of the garage was a desk. It was cluttered with tools and cans of paint. Nothing out of the ordinary. There was a bicycle leaning against the wall. A red helmet was affixed to the bike seat. And next to the bike, on the cement floor—

A dark green toolbox. Ah-ha!

I turned to make another quick scan across the street. A car went by, but other than that, no one was in sight.

I stood up. As soon as I did, I realized my mistake. There was a window on the side of the garage, and I could clearly see Mrs. Rodriguez! She was only a few feet away, hanging clothes on a clothesline in her back yard!

Which meant that if she turned, she would see me!

Then I'd *really* be in a lot of trouble.

I dropped to my knees again, hoping that she wouldn't come into the garage. Time dragged on. My heart pounded, and I counted out seconds in my head.

One thousand one . . . One thousand two . . . One thousand three . . . One thousand four . . . .

When I reached sixty, I stood up very slowly and peered out the window into the back yard. Mrs. Rodriguez was gone.

Whew! That had been a close one.

I turned and looked at the green toolbox on the other side of the garage. Then I gave one glance behind me before tiptoeing quickly across the cement to the toolbox. I knelt down and opened it.

Inside was a brown envelope. There were strange markings all over it, like a language I couldn't understand. It sure didn't look familiar.

But when I opened it up, I recognized the language right away. It was plain English, and easy to read.

And as I read, I realized for the first time that I was in real danger. Not just me, however.

The entire world was in danger! In my hands, I held the secret plans of an alien invasion to take over the world!

11

As I continued reading the master plans, I realized that I was trembling. I was becoming more and more horrified by the moment.

The master plan was this: aliens from a planet called 430-X were going to invade Earth and take all of our water! Through some sort of process that I didn't understand, these aliens would be able to gather up all of the water on our planet and compress it into a single, fifty-gallon container. They would take it back to 430-X, decompress it, and use it for themselves!

I know it sounded like something out of a science fiction book, but it was true. The aliens had sent androids—people like Mrs. Rodriguez—to Earth to prepare the way. According to the plans, there were hundreds of androids living in Arizona, quietly working to get ready for the alien invasion!

It was a horrible, horrible thought. If the aliens succeeded, the people of Earth wouldn't have any water left. No one can live without water!

Now I had my proof. I knew all along that something wasn't right. But what could I do?

First thing, I would tell Arielle. She's super-smart. If I could convince her of what was going on, she would know what to do.

I placed the master plans back into the toolbox. I had thought about taking them with me, but if Mrs. Rodriguez came out to look at them for whatever reason, she would discover that they were missing . . . and the first person she would suspect would be me. No, it would be better to leave the master plans where they were for the time being. Besides . . . I knew enough about the aliens' plans that Arielle would *have* to believe me. She would know that there was just no way I could make up something like this.

I slipped out of the garage and once again ducked down to creep close to Mrs. Rodriguez's house. When I reached the bushes on the other side of the yard, I ducked into them and emerged on the other side. I waited and watched for a moment, just to be sure that I hadn't been spotted. It was a busy neighborhood, and I could see a few people in their yards, but thankfully, nobody looked like they were paying attention to me.

Then I leapt out of the bushes and broke into a run. The day was warm and it wasn't long before I had broken out into a sweat. But I wasn't going to stop until I reached Arielle's home.

Finally, after what seemed like an hour (it was really only five minutes) I made it to the small, white house where Arielle lived. I sprinted across the grass and bounded up to the front door.

"Arielle!" I exclaimed, pounding on the door. "Arielle?!?! Are you home?!?!"

The door opened, and Arielle stood in the doorway. "What's up with you?" she asked, stepping onto the porch and closing the door behind her. "My dad is taking a nap. If you wake him up, he's going to be madder than a wet hen!"

"You're not going to believe what I found out!" I said. "About Mrs. Rodriguez!"

"Oh, brother," Arielle said with a roll of her eyes. "Here we go again. You still think she's a robot?"

I shook my head. "Not a robot!" I said. "An android! She was sent here—along with a bunch of other androids—by aliens from a planet called 430-X! They are planning to invade and steal all of Earth's water!"

Arielle took a step back, like I had the flu and she was afraid of catching it.

"That is the craziest thing you've ever said," Arielle stated flatly. "Are you sure you're feeling okay?"

"I'm fine!" I said. "You've got to believe me! I was over at Mrs. Rodriguez's house and found the master plans! I read the whole thing myself. The aliens have sent the androids here to build a secret base for them. You've got to believe me, Arielle! I'm telling you the truth!"

"I believe," Arielle said quietly.

"You . . . you *do?*" I replied.

"I believe . . . you're out of your mind," she finished. Then she opened the front door and stepped inside. "Now, I have better things to do than listen to crazy stories about aliens and androids. I'll see you tomorrow in school." She closed the door, leaving me standing, bewildered, on her front porch.

Well, if Arielle won't believe me, Joey will, I thought. *He won't think that I'm making it up.*

I leapt off the porch and broke into a run again, this time heading four blocks over to Joey's house. He was outside, mowing the lawn. When he saw me, he shut off the mower. I ran up to him, out of breath.

"Joey! You've got to believe me!" I gasped.

"Hey, slow down, slow down," he said. "Take it easy. You're going to choke. Now . . . believe you about what?"

"I was right all along," I huffed, still gasping for breath. "Mrs. Rodriguez isn't a robot, though . . . she's an android! She was sent here by aliens who want to take over the world!"

"What?!?!" he exclaimed, raising an eyebrow.

"Let me explain," I said. "Let me tell you everything, and then decide if I'm telling you the truth."

"Okay," he replied.

I told him everything . . . how I'd gone to Mrs. Rodriguez's house and heard her talking in a mechanical voice, and how I found the tool box with the master plans. All the while Joey listened intently.

When I finished, I eyed him cautiously. "You've just got to believe me," I added. "I've never lied to you before, ever. And I'm not lying now."

"I . . . guess I believe you, Shelby . . . but you yourself have to realize that your story sounds crazy."

"I know it does," I agreed, "but I heard Mrs. Rodriguez with my own ears. I saw the master plans with my own eyes."

"Where are they?"

"I left them in the toolbox. I didn't want to take them in case Mrs. Rodriguez wanted to look at them. If she saw that the plans were missing, I would be the first person that she would suspect."

"Can we go look?" he asked.

"Sure," I said. "We'll just have to be careful that no one sees us."

"Then let's go," Joey said. "I've got to see this. I can finish the lawn when I get back."

And so, the two of us headed over to Mrs. Rodriguez's house. I felt better knowing that Joey believed me. If Joey believed me, then maybe I could get Arielle to believe me. All I had to do was show Joey the master plan, and let him read it for himself. But as we rounded the corner and headed toward Mrs. Rodriguez's home, I saw something that made me realize that this wasn't going to be as easy as I thought.

12

Mrs. Rodriguez's garage door was closed.

"Oh no!" I said, stopping on the sidewalk.

"What?" Joey asked, as he, too, stopped walking. "What's wrong?"

I pointed. "Her garage door is closed," I said. "It was open earlier. That's how I got inside."

"Is there another way in?" he asked.

I shook my head. "I don't know. But if there is, it's probably not a good idea. You still believe me, don't you?"

"Yeah, I do. But I'd really like to read the master plans."

We stood for a moment, basking in the hot sun. There wasn't a single cloud in the sky.

"I have another idea," I said. "We could sneak up behind her house and see what she's up to."

"You mean . . . *spy on her?*" Joey said.

"It's not really spying," I replied. "She's not a human. She's an android."

"I don't know," Joey said. "That doesn't sound like such a good idea."

"Oh, come on," I replied.

"Why the back of the house?" Joey asked. "Why don't we sneak up in the front where we can hide behind the bushes?"

"That's how I was caught last time," I answered. "Some lady across the street saw me and called Mrs. Rodriguez. If we sneak around the back, we can duck down beneath the windows. Maybe we can find out more."

Joey started to protest, but I had already started moving. He had no choice but to follow me.

We darted around a few shrubs and ran up to Mrs. Rodriguez's house. From there, we fell to our hands and knees and crawled around to the back of her home. Thankfully, there was a tight row of shrubs growing close to her house, just like there was in the front yard. We were completely hidden, unless Mrs. Rodriguez came outside.

And I sure didn't want that to happen.

When we were beneath the kitchen window, I could hear the clatter of dishes in the sink. But more importantly, I could hear a voice . . . the same, droning, mechanical voice that I'd heard earlier!

I turned to look at Joey's face. His eyes were wide, and he held an expression of complete disbelief. He *had* to believe me now . . . especially when he heard what Mrs. Rodriguez was saying.

" . . . *and final preparations are under way,*" she was saying. *"The people of Earth haven't any idea what is about to happen."*

Joey gasped out loud, and I turned and placed a hand over his mouth. Then I leaned closer to him, my lips right next to his ear.

"See what I mean?" I whispered. Joey nodded, his eyes still popping out of his head. *"We've got to get out of here and get help,"* I said quietly. *"Let's go tell our parents."*

That seemed like the best idea. I knew that my mom and dad wouldn't believe me alone, but if Joey backed up my story, well, they would probably listen.

Wrong.

We snuck away from Mrs. Rodriguez's home and raced to my house. My mom and dad had just returned home from work, and were in the kitchen. Joey and I, out of breath from running, stormed into the house.

"Whoah, whoah, whoah," my dad said with a laugh. "Where's the fire?"

"It's not a fire!" I gasped. "It's aliens! They are going to take over the earth and steal our water!"

"She's telling the truth!" Joey wheezed. "We aren't making this up! Our teacher, Mrs. Rodriguez, is an android, and she's been sent here by aliens from another planet to help with the invasion. They want to steal all of our water and take it back to their planet!"

Mom and Dad stared at us for a moment. Suddenly, they both burst out laughing. They thought we were joking!

"That's funny," Mom said. "Is that a story that you're working on for school?"

"It's not a story!" I insisted. "It's for real! You've got to believe us!"

"I'll believe a lot of things," Mom said, "but that's not one of them. I always knew you had a good imagination, Shelby. But this takes the cake!"

"We're telling the truth, Mrs. Crusado," Joey said. "I didn't believe it at first. But Shelby's right. We've got to do something!"

"If you want to do something, go help unload the groceries from the car," Mom said.

"I'm serious, Mom!" I protested.

But it was no use. My mom and dad weren't going to believe us. Not only that, but they made us unload all of the groceries from the back seat of Mom's car.

Then we ran to Joey's house and told his mom. Her reaction was the same: she didn't believe us. After trying to talk to her for a few minutes, we realized that it was hopeless and we went outside and sat on the porch.

"We need to get some proof," I said as we sat on the steps of the front porch. "We need to have something for everyone to see. Then they would believe us."

"But what?" Joey asked. "The master plans? Mrs. Rodriguez closed her garage door. She might have even taken the plans out of the toolbox."

We thought long and hard, but nothing came to mind. Soon, the screen door whisked open, and Joey's Mom stood in the doorway.

"Joey," she said, "have you seen the masking tape? It was on the kitchen table this morning, and I need it."

"Yeah, I was using it to fix my model airplane. I left it in my bedroom on my dresser. Sorry."

Joey's mom vanished . . . leaving me with a great idea.

"Joey, that's it!" I exclaimed. "I think I know how we can prove once and for all that Mrs. Rodriguez is an android!"

13

"What?!?!" Joey exclaimed. "You've got to tell me!"

"The masking tape gave me an idea," I said.

"How?" asked Joey. "What has masking tape got to do with it?"

"Not masking tape," I said. *"Recording* tape. We need to record Mrs. Rodriguez talking in that strange voice. If we can do that, we'll have the proof we need!"

"I have a cassette tape recorder in my room!" Joey said, snapping his fingers. "It's only about the size of a paperback book, too. All we would have to do is find a place where we could hide it without Mrs. Rodriguez seeing it!"

We thought about it for a while and decided the best thing to do would be to put the cassette recorder on Mrs. Rodriguez's desk just before lunch. She usually stays in her room while the rest of us go to the cafeteria. That way, if she had any communication with other androids or aliens, we would have the conversation on tape.

"I hope we don't get caught," Joey said. "We would get into a lot of trouble."

"Yeah," I said, "but think about it. I wouldn't ever record someone else's conversation secretly. But we're not talking about a human, here. We're talking about Mrs. Rodriguez—an android—who is part of a plan to take over the world."

"I guess you're right," Joey said. "But I still feel funny doing it."

"Don't worry," I said. "We'll get Mrs. Rodriguez on tape. Then people will have to believe us. We might be able to stop the alien invasion, if we act quick enough."

"When do you want to try it?" Joey asked.

"We don't have any time to lose. I didn't hear when the aliens are supposed to invade, but I know it's going to be soon. We need to get your recorder on Mrs. Rodriguez's desk tomorrow."

"Okay," Joey said. "I'll bring it to school."

The next morning, I met Joey on the playground.

"Did you remember the tape recorder?" I asked.

Joey responded by reaching into his backpack and pulling out a black and silver cassette recorder. "I even put in fresh batteries and a brand new tape," he said.

"Good thinking," I replied. "I just know that this is going to work."

During class, I kept a careful eye on Mrs. Rodriguez. Strangely enough, I felt she was doing the same thing to *me* . . . watching me. Wondering what I was thinking.

Then it was lunchtime, and we went to work on our plan. All of our classmates headed to the cafeteria, but Joey and I stayed behind.

"Mrs. Rodriguez," I said, "I have a question about our math homework."

She was happy to help, and she showed me the equation on the blackboard. Meanwhile, Joey carefully placed the cassette recorder on her desk and concealed it beneath a few pieces of paper.

"Thank you, Mrs. Rodriguez," I said, after she was finished showing me the math equation.

"You're welcome. I'm not all that bad for a robot, huh?"

I shuddered, and I hoped she didn't see it. I know that she was only joking . . . but the fact was, I knew the truth.

My teacher was an android.

And Joey and I were going to prove it.

"Come on, Shelby," Joey said. "Let's head down to the cafeteria and have lunch."

We left the classroom and walked down the hall. I turned around to make sure that Mrs. Rodriguez wasn't looking or following us. She wasn't.

"That was pretty easy," Joey said.

"I wish I could be a fly on the wall," I said, "and listen to her conversation. I'll bet she's talking with aliens right now!"

"Well, having that tape recorder on the desk sort of *is* like being a fly on the wall," Joey said. "If she's talking to aliens or other androids, we'll know about it."

Retrieving the cassette recorder at the end of the day wasn't difficult. When the bell rang, a half dozen students swarmed Mrs. Rodriguez's desk to ask her questions. Joey was able to pick up the tape recorder without anyone even knowing.

"Got it!" he whispered to me as we walked out of class.

"Turn it on!" I said. *"I've got to hear what she says!"*

"Let's wait until we're somewhere safer," Joey replied. *"Let's go out to the playground where no one else can hear."*

We walked down the hall and out the front doors. There were a few kids hanging around the playground, but nobody was near the swing set. We hurried over and sat in separate swings.

"Okay, hang on a second," Joey said. "I've got to rewind this thing."

I waited anxiously as the cassette rewound. All the while, I wondered what was on the tape. Sure, there was always a chance that there wasn't anything on it at all. But I was hopeful, anyway.

"Okay, here we go," Joey finally said. I was so excited that I got out of my swing and stood next to Joey so I could hear better. Joey pressed the 'play' button, and we listened.

Tape hiss. That's all we heard. And a shuffling of papers. More tape hiss.

My hopes began to fade. I was really hoping that we'd caught Mrs. Rodriguez on tape, saying something that would prove our story.

"Rats," I said. "That's a bummer. I thought that we would—"

"Shhh!" Joey said, placing a finger to his lips. "I think there's something there! Listen!"

My heart skipped a beat, and I held my breath.

I listened.

Joey listened.

Suddenly, we could hear the mechanical, electronic-sounding voice of Mrs. Rodriguez! She was speaking, and we'd caught every word of what she said!

But her words chilled us to the bone, and as we listened, Joey and I were filled with a fear like we'd never known.

14

What we had on tape was incredible.

Mrs. Rodriguez was talking about the alien plans, and while we couldn't tell who she was talking to, we sure knew what she was saying. She was talking about how the master plan was coming together fine. There were parts on the tape that we couldn't hear very well, and she seemed far away. But other times her voice was as clear as the sky, and we could hear every word.

"Yes, it's fine," she was saying. *"The base is nearing completion. It's hidden away in a place right here in a state the humans call Arizona."*

Joey and I looked at each other and gasped. We listened as she explained how other androids had built secret caverns somewhere in Arizona that would be used to hold alien spacecraft.

"This is incredible," Joey said. "I just can't believe it. And I can't believe you found those master plans."

"Now we have our proof," I said. "Now, everyone will have to believe us."

We kept listening. There were long gaps in Mrs. Rodriguez's conversation when she was listening to whoever she was talking to. She talked about her spacecraft, and how it was safe in an old warehouse not far from her home.

"Wow," I said. "Mrs. Rodriguez has her own spacecraft. That's cool!"

"I wonder who she's talking to?" Joey said. "I mean . . . do you think she is talking to an alien, or another android?"

"There's no way of telling," I said. "The important thing is that we have her conversation on tape. Now we can do something about it! Maybe we could send the tape to the president! He needs to know about this! Then he can send jet fighters and the army to stop the aliens!"

Joey shook his head. "That sounds like a good idea, but we need to convince some people here, first. If we sent the tape to the president, he'd probably think that it was sent by a couple of kids playing a joke."

"Yeah, you're right," I said, heaving a sigh of disappointment.

We continued listening to Mrs. Rodriguez on the tape. Some of what she was saying was really technical, and I didn't know what it meant. Other things were very clear.

And one thing in particular was clearest of all.

Near the end of her conversation, we heard her say exactly when the alien invasion would take place.

"... *tomorrow*," she was saying, *"the secret base will be complete. Then the invasion can begin!"*

Oh no! Aliens from 430-X were going to invade Earth ... the very next day!

15

We didn't have a lot of time.

"Okay, first things first," I said. "Let's take the tape to my parents. When they hear Mrs. Rodriguez, I know they'll believe me. Dad will know what to do."

"Good idea," Joey said, sliding off the swing that he'd been seated on. He stopped the tape recorder and slipped it into his backpack. "Let's go."

We walked to my house, all the while talking about what we'd heard. It was all so incredible.

"This is like the stuff from movies," Joey said.

"I kind of wish it was," I replied. "When you think about what could happen, it's pretty scary."

"I wonder if anybody else knows," Joey said.

"Well, other androids, that's for sure," I replied. "Who knows how many there could be. In fact, there might even be other android teachers at our school!"

"I'll bet Principal Walinski is an android," Joey said. "I've always thought he was from outer space."

I laughed. Principal Walinski wears really odd glasses that make him look really geeky. He's a really nice guy, but he looks like a giant bug with his glasses on.

When we got to my house, Mom and Dad were still at work, so we sat in the living room and listened to the tape again. Even though we'd already heard it once, it was still chilling to hear the robot-like words of Mrs. Rodriguez, explaining the diabolical plan.

Finally, Dad's car pulled into the driveway.

"Quick!" I said to Joey. "Rewind the tape so Dad can hear everything right from the beginning!"

The tape finished rewinding just as Dad came through the front door.

"Hey guys," he said with a smile. Then, noticing our expressions, he froze. The smile faded. "Okay," he said. "You guys look worried. What's up?"

"Dad . . . sit down. We have something that you have to hear."

Dad sat down on the sofa next to me. "Okay," he said. "What is it you want me to hear?"

I figured that it would be best if Dad heard the words of Mrs. Rodriguez for himself. "Go ahead, Joey."

Joey reached out and turned on the tape recorder. When the strange voice began, I turned to Dad. *That's Mrs. Rodriguez,"* I said quietly. *"Listen."*

Dad listened intently, his brow knotted. In the parts where Mrs. Rodriguez was silent, we tried to explain a little more about what was going on. When the tape was finished, Joey turned off the recorder.

"Well?" I asked Dad. "What do we do?"

"What do you mean?" Dad replied.

"The tape," I said. "The government needs to hear this! Who do we take the tape to?"

Suddenly, Dad exploded with a fit of laughter. "Oh, cut it out, you guys," he said, standing up. "It's a great joke, and you did a very good job with that computerized voice."

"Computerized voice?!?!" I gasped. "But . . . but it's not! It's real! That's the voice of Mrs. Rodriguez! Didn't you hear? She even has her own spacecraft hidden in a warehouse!"

Again, Dad laughed.

"Honest, Mr. Crusado!" Joey exclaimed. "This isn't a joke!"

But Dad wouldn't listen. He just shook his head and walked away. "Good grief," he said, as he walked down the hall. "Aliens! Androids!" He laughed some more, then disappeared into his study.

"So much for getting anyone to believe us," Joey said.

"I really thought that we had all the proof we needed," I said, pointing at the tape recorder. "What will it take for people to start believing us?"

"What about Arielle?" Joey asked.

"We can try," I said, "but I think she's mad at me. I went to her house yesterday and told her about the master plan that I'd found, and she told me to quit wasting her time."

"Well, now it's different," Joey said. "Now we have Mrs. Rodriguez on tape. Let's go over to her house and play it for Arielle. The more people we can get to believe us, the better."

"We haven't had much luck so far," I said. "I guess it's worth a shot."

Joey picked up the tape recorder and we left, heading for Arielle's house. We were silent as we walked. I was thinking about what we could do to get people to believe us, so we could warn everyone. The aliens had to be stopped, but if we couldn't get anyone to listen to us, it would be hopeless.

We reached Arielle's house and I knocked on the door. No answer.

"That's odd," I said. "She's usually home by now."

"But she wasn't in class today," Joey said. "Maybe her family went somewhere."

I knocked again, but no one came to the door.

"Wait a minute," I said, looking down. Between the screen and the door was a folded slip of paper. I opened up the screen door a tiny bit and picked it up.

"What is it?" Joey asked as I unfolded the paper.

"It's a note," I replied. But when I started reading, I gasped in horror.

"What?" Joey asked. "What's it say?"

"It's a note from Arielle!" I exclaimed. *"She's been kidnapped by the androids!"*

16

I began to read the note out loud, from the beginning.

"Please help me. My name is Arielle, and I've been kidnapped by androids, sent here by aliens from the planet 430-X. They have taken me because they think that I know about their master plan to take over the world. I'm not sure, but I think they're taking me to 430-X so that I won't tell anyone about . . ."

"Keep reading!" Joey prodded.

I shook my head. "That's all there is," I replied. "She must not have had time to finish her note."

"Kidnapped," Joey said. "I can't believe it."

"And worst of all, no one else will believe us. Dad didn't believe us when we played the tape for him. He'll never believe us if we show him this note."

"But what are we going to do?" Joey asked.

I read the note again, silently this time. Arielle was my friend, and now she was gone.

"We need to do something," I said. "What if we went over to Mrs. Rodriguez's house? You know . . . we could tell her that we know all about the plans for the invasion, and if they don't bring Arielle back, we'll go to the police."

Joey shook his head. "I don't think that'll work," he said. "It will probably just get us kidnapped, too."

I sat down on the porch, and Joey sat down next to me.

"Well, we know that the androids have been sent here by the aliens," Joey said. "And they're planning to invade tomorrow and take all of Earth's water. And we know that their base is hidden somewhere in Arizona."

"And we know that our teacher is involved in the whole thing," I said.

"And Arielle has been kidnapped and taken to 430-X, because they think she knows of the master plan," Joey said.

I shook my head. "That's our fault," I said with a sigh.

"Hey, not entirely," Joey offered. "I mean . . . we've done everything we could to get people to believe us. Nobody has."

"And nobody will," I said. "We've got to do something. If no one will believe us, we'll have to do something on our own."

"But what?" Joey said in exasperation. "If nobody is going to believe us, what can two kids in Scottsdale do?"

I turned and looked Joey in the eye.

"I know what we'll do," I said confidently.

"You . . . you do?" Joey replied.

I nodded. "Think about it. What did Mrs. Rodriguez say on the tape?"

Joey looked away, deep in thought. "Well, she talked about the invasion, and how the base is here in Arizona."

"Yeah," I agreed. "But what else? Remember what she said?"

"She said something about . . . about—"

"About her spaceship that's hidden in a warehouse not far away."

Joey's eyes just about popped out of his head. His jaw fell. "You're . . . you're not thinking—"

"That's *exactly* what I'm thinking," I said with a nod. "We're going to find that spaceship. We're going to find it . . . and then we're going to find Arielle."

Ready or not, our space adventure was about to begin.

17

Although we knew we didn't have much time, we decided to wait until the following morning to begin our search for the spaceship. It would be Saturday, so we'd have a lot of time if we got up early.

And finding the spacecraft might not be very easy. Joey came to my house early in the morning, and we made our plans as we sat on the porch. The sun was rising steadily, and it was going to be another hot, dry day. A typical September day in Arizona.

"We don't have too much to go on," I said. "All Mrs. Rodriguez said was that it was hidden in a warehouse not far from where she lives. We'll have to start there. The good thing is, there aren't very many warehouses nearby."

We set out, not really knowing exactly what we were in for. I mean . . . two kids can't just go barging into warehouses to look for spaceships!

But we figured that wherever her spacecraft was located, it would probably be a place where there weren't a lot of people around. Like maybe an abandoned warehouse or building.

"There's one over on Willow street," Joey said.

"I guess that's as good of a place as any to start," I replied, and we set out. Willow street was only a few blocks away, and it didn't take us long to get there.

"It doesn't look very big," Joey said.

"Yeah, but we have no idea how big the spaceship is," I said. "Come on. Let's go look in the windows."

We walked across the empty parking lot. At one time the building had been used to store machinery, but it's been closed for years.

And when we got closer and peered through the windows, it was easy to see that there wasn't a spacecraft inside. Matter of fact, there wasn't a single thing inside at all. The building was completely empty.

"Rats," I said. I was hoping my good luck charm would work better than this.

"One down," Joey said. "How about that big brick building on Fourth street?"

"Might as well check it out," I said, and we started walking again. Fourth street was a little farther away, and it took us almost fifteen minutes to reach it.

"There it is, over there," I said, pointing to the big brick building at the end of Fourth street. The building didn't look like much, but it was good-sized. If I was an android and needed to hide my spaceship, it would be a great place.

We walked up to the building. Some of the windows were boarded up, but others weren't. I gazed through one of them, cupping my hands around my face to block the sun's glare behind me.

"Rats," I said. "Nothing but a few stacks of crates and a single car." I drew back and began thinking about other places where we could look.

"Wait, a minute," Joey said. His face was still pressed to the glass, and his hands were cupped around his face.

"What?" I said, once again placing my face against the glass and peering inside. "What do you see?"

"The same thing you see," Joey replied. "A car. But it looks kind of out-of-place, sitting in the middle of a big, empty building."

Joey was right. It did look kind of strange.

But it certainly wasn't a spaceship!

Joey drew back from the window and walked to a big, gray door. He grasped the knob and pushed. The door opened.

"Not even locked," he said, and he stepped into the building.

I wasn't sure if it was a good idea or not, but it was a little too late now. I followed Joey inside, and we walked toward the car.

The inside of the building was spacious, bigger than a gymnasium, with a very high ceiling. I wondered what it had been used for. Near the walls were stacks of crates that were piled ten feet high.

The car sat in the middle of the building. It was an ordinary Chevrolet. Red, with shiny, silver wheel rims.

"See?" I said. "Just a car."

Without another word, Joey opened the car door.

"What are you doing?!?!" I exclaimed. "That doesn't belong to you!"

"Hang on," Joey said. "I've got a hunch."

"You're going to have a hunch in jail," I said.

"No, really, Shelby . . . hang on a second." He sat down in the driver's seat. "There's something strange about this car."

I watched as he fumbled with a few knobs and radio buttons. Then I grew impatient.

"Come *on*," I urged. "We're going to get into a lot of trouble if you don't—"

Suddenly, there was a loud electrical whirring noise. Joey sprang out of the car and leapt away, leaving the door open.

We watched . . . and what happened next was beyond unbelievable.

18

The car began to change!

Right before our eyes, the car began to change shape. First, the doors, hood, and trunk opened like a big flower. Then they twisted around. The car reared back, and more things began to spring out and fold around. Metal screeched and scraped.

"Holy smokes," Joey breathed. "It's transforming."

Joey was right. The car was indeed changing into something totally different, into something that was no longer a car. Within minutes, the vehicle had completely changed.

It was now a spaceship.

All we could do was stare. The craft had a clear glass canopy. Beneath the glass was a cockpit with two seats. There was a control panel with all sorts of blinking lights and dials. The back of the spaceship was engulfed by a large, powerful-looking engine and two large rocket thrusters that were as big around as garbage cans. The thing was unlike anything else I'd ever seen.

Well, maybe in the movies. I certainly hadn't seen one of these things buzzing around Scottsdale!

"We found it," Joey breathed as he cautiously walked toward the spaceship. *"We really found it."*

I followed after Joey, and we walked up to the strange space vehicle. I glanced nervously around to make sure that no one was watching. The last thing we needed was Mrs. Rodriguez or someone else catching us here.

There were several buttons on the side of the spacecraft. Joey pressed one, but nothing happened. But when he pressed another, the glass canopy raised up and back, sort of like a convertible.

Joey shot me a smirk. "Want to go for a ride?" he asked.

I wasn't so sure. I mean . . . it was a spaceship. I don't even know how to drive a car, let alone a spacecraft!

"Are you sure?" I asked him. "Do you really think you can drive this thing?"

"You don't *drive* spaceships," he said. "You *pilot* them. And I think we can figure it out."

Without another word, he raised his leg and slipped into the spacecraft. "Climb in the other side," he said.

I walked around the craft and got in.

"This canopy has to close somehow," he said, inspecting the buttons on the control panel. "Ah. Here it is." He flicked a lever and the glass canopy lowered back into place.

Well, it took us a while, but Joey finally figured out how to operate the spaceship. The rocket engines roared to life. Soon, we were rising to the ceiling, then lowering back down again. He moved the spacecraft forward, then back, then around the building in a circle, being careful not to bump into the walls or the ceiling. Once, we bumped into a stack of crates, but none of them fell.

And it was really fun, too. I was nervous at first—so nervous that I thought I was going to be sick. But Joey took it real easy, learning more and more about the spaceship, seeing what it could do.

But I couldn't believe what we were about to do. We'd actually found Mrs. Rodriguez's spaceship, which was pretty incredible in itself . . . but now we were about to set off to a planet to rescue our friend!

First, however, we had to find a way to get the contraption out of the building.

There was a series of double doors near the front of the structure, but they weren't big enough to get the craft through. On the opposite side of the building was a big garage-type door . . . one that rolled up automatically, like my garage door at home. That looked like it would be big enough. After all . . . the spaceship had made it *inside*. There must be a way to get it out.

Joey lowered the craft to the ground. "Go and open that big door," he said as he pressed a button on the panel in front of him. "There should be a green button on the wall near the row of light switches."

I climbed out of the spaceship and walked over to the big garage door. Sure enough, there was a series of buttons next to the light switches. A green one was labeled 'open'. I pressed it, and the wide aluminum door began to rise. Sunlight poured in, brighter and brighter as the door rose higher and higher.

"Come on!" Joey hollered from the spacecraft. "Let's get out of here before we're spotted!"

I raced back to the ship and leapt inside. The glass canopy lowered and locked in place, and Joey guided the craft off the ground.

"Outer space, here we come!" I exclaimed, and the spaceship lurched forward, out of the building and into the bright sunshine.

"Now we get to see what this thing really can do," Joey said.

"Aren't there any seat belts in this thing?" I asked, looking around.

"There should be." He inspected the panel again. "Here we go." He pressed a button, and instantly a snake-like cord came up from behind us, wrapping our waists and pulling us snugly to the seats.

"Much better," I said. "Just in case."

"Hang on," Joey said.

Suddenly, we were rocketing skyward at a speed that was incredible. Our spacecraft was pointing almost straight up, and when I looked to the side, I could see the city of

Scottsdale falling away rapidly. I wondered if anyone on the ground could see us.

Right behind us, the roar of the rocket-propelled motor was deafening. Joey yelled something to me, but I couldn't understand what he said.

And as we rose higher and higher, the color of the sky changed. It went from a bright, rich blue, to a deep, dark blue. The higher we traveled, the darker the sky became. Soon, it was almost black. Stars began to appear. I looked to my side beyond the glass and was surprised to see the entire shape of the earth below me.

But ahead of us was something else.

The moon.

Joey was trying to steer us away from it, but the spacecraft didn't seem to respond. Meanwhile, the big silvery disc loomed larger and larger.

"What's wrong?" I shouted above the roaring rocket behind us.

"It won't steer!" Joey replied. *"I can't control it!"*

"We're going to crash into the moon!" I shrieked. *"Do something!"*

"I'm trying! I'm trying!"

Ahead, the moon rushed toward us like an aluminum desert. We were only seconds away from impact.

"There's nothing I can do!" he screamed. *"Hang on! We're going to crash!"*

I placed my hands on the panel and pushed back. Then I closed my eyes . . . and waited for the worst.

19

I don't know if it was something that Joey did, or maybe just pure, dumb luck . . . but at the last possible moment, the spacecraft veered violently to the right. We avoided hitting the moon by only a few feet!

Joey cut the rocket engine and the roar died away. I was shaking, and so was he. That had been a close call . . . too close for comfort.

"I thought you knew what you were doing," I said. My voice trembled.

"I thought so, too," Joey replied. "But this thing steers different in space than it did on Earth. It must have something to do with the Earth's gravity."

Now that we were out of danger—at least for the moment—I took a look around. What I saw beyond the glass canopy was spectacular.

To the right of me was the moon, big and glowing and bright. We were so close to it that I could make out hundreds and hundreds of craters and the shadows they cast. Ahead and above us, the dark curtain of space was everywhere, dotted with thousands of stars. They looked odd, though. They didn't twinkle like they do when you see them from Earth.

"There has got to be an onboard navigational system on this thing," Joey said, gazing at the control panel.

"You mean, like some sort of map or something?" I asked.

"Yeah," Joey replied. "My dad has a thing in his car that tells him exactly where he is. That way, he can program where he wants to go, and the unit tells him how to get there. A spaceship like this would probably have one of those, too."

There was a small computer screen right between us, but there wasn't anything to see. Joey fiddled with a series of buttons and keys beneath it, finally succeeding in turning it on. The screen winked and turned blue.

"This has to be it," he said, still working with the unit.

"Just watch what you're doing so you don't steer us into Mars," I said.

Suddenly, the computer screen flickered. A list of numbers and letters appeared.

"Got it!" Joey said. "Look at that!"

I squinted at the screen. "What is it?"

"Coordinates. These are all places that the craft can be programmed to go. I'll bet if I scroll down, I'll find the planet we're looking for."

It took a couple of minutes, but Joey finally found 430-X. He pressed a key and the screen went blank. Then the words *PLEASE WAIT A MOMENT* appeared.

"It's programming itself," Joey said. "The coordinates are probably loading into the navigation system."

Soon another message began flashing on the screen. It read: *PLEASE PREPARE FOR LIGHT SPEED TRAVEL*.

"How do you prepare for light speed travel?" I asked.

"We hang on tight," Joey said.

As soon as he said those words, the spacecraft lunged forward so violently that I was pinned to the seat. It felt like my eyeballs were pushing back into my brain. Beyond the spaceship, the stars had turned into streaks of white. I was barely aware that the rocket engine behind us had exploded to life, and now we were roaring through outer space, faster than any other human beings have ever traveled.

"If nobody believed us about the androids and the aliens, they sure aren't going to believe *this!*" I said, my voice quaking as the ship went faster and faster.

The ship traveled deeper and deeper into space. Stars streaked by like insects. Still, we kept traveling farther and farther into the depths of space.

A bajillion questions began going through my mind.

What is 430-X going to be like? I wondered. *What are the aliens going to look like? How are we going to find*

Arielle? What if we're captured? Will we ever make it back to Earth? Can two kids really stop an alien invasion?

I had to force myself not to think about these things. There was too much danger, too many things that could go wrong. The first thing we needed to do was make it to 430-X. Then we would plan from there.

Soon, the spaceship began to slow on its own. Up ahead, a single pinpoint of light grew larger and larger.

"That must be it," I said. "That must be 430-X."

The ship slowed some more. Indeed, we were approaching a planet. It was sort of greenish-blue, similar to what Earth looks like from space.

But something else came into view.

Spaceships.

Dozens of them, lined up in space, hanging steadily, unmoving. And as we drew nearer, it was easy to see that these weren't ordinary spaceships.

They were warships . . . readying for the invasion of Earth.

20

During our journey through space, the ship had commandeered itself. Now Joey regained control and slowed the craft as we approached the line of warships lined up in space.

"What do we do?" I asked quietly.

"I say we just keep going like normal. We're in an alien spacecraft, so we won't look out of place or anything."

He had a point.

More questions whirled through my head. *What do the aliens look like? Are they tall with six arms? Are they short and green? And what is their planet like? Is there air on 430-X, like there is on Earth?* I was really having a lot of second thoughts about what we had done. There were a lot of things that we hadn't thought about when we found Mrs. Rodriguez's spaceship and set out across the galaxy.

Joey guided the craft below the line of warships. Most of them appeared to be about twice the size of our craft, but a few of them were the same size.

Beyond the waiting warships was planet 430-X. It glowed blue-green, with long, white swirls that looked like they might be clouds.

"Hang on," Joey said. "It might get bumpy when we enter their atmosphere."

"How do you know?" I asked. "You've never been to another planet before."

"I see this stuff on television all the time," Joey replied confidently. "It always gets bumpy when a spaceship re-enters the atmosphere from outer space."

And he was right, too. The spaceship began to bounce up and down and all around. It's a good thing that we were strapped in tight, otherwise we would have been tossed all around the craft.

Soon, the bouncing stopped, and the spacecraft steadied. Joey piloted it toward 430-X, which was looming closer and closer by the second. As we approached, the sky around us went from black to dark, dark blue. Then it lightened to a rich, glacier blue.

"This might be just like Earth," I said, "with a blue sky and everything. Maybe the aliens look just like us, too."

"I think we'll be finding out soon enough," Joey said. He was really doing a good job of steering the spacecraft—for someone who had never operated one before.

"Look," I said, pointing. "That looks like some kind of ocean, only it's green." Below us was a large, smooth, lime-colored expanse. It appeared to be a body of water, only a different color than what we had back on Earth.

"And there are mountains, too," Joey pointed out. "Right over there."

The experience was exciting, but a little scary, too. And I still wondered how we were going to find Arielle. Maybe they hadn't even brought her here. Maybe she was being held captive on one of the warships that we passed.

"What's that over there?" I said, pointing to the left of Joey. He steered the craft in that direction.

Beneath us appeared to be a city of some sort. I could pick out what looked like buildings and other structures.

"Let's travel around a bit before we land," Joey said. "Maybe there are other cities. And besides . . . we might not want to land in the city right away. It might be best to land someplace where no one will see us."

"Good idea," I said. "We don't even know if we can breathe on this planet."

As we proceeded closer and closer to the surface of 430-X, I realized I was wrong about the ocean. It wasn't an ocean at all . . . but a huge, green desert that encompassed a large part of the entire planet. Near the edge were trees of some sort, but we were still too far to see what they looked like.

We skimmed across the green desert, heading for the distant tree line. "We'll land there," Joey said. "It doesn't look like there are any aliens around."

The craft raced across the strange, green plain. High above was a yellow sun, just like Earth's. The sky was blue, but the clouds were a pinkish-red color. They looked very different from the clouds you would see on our planet.

Up ahead, the trees came into view, but they didn't look like normal trees at all. These trees were purple with long, gold leaves that shined in the bright sun. Some trees had shiny needles, like pine trees, only the needles on these trees were a lot longer.

"This looks like a good place to land," Joey said.

He slowed the spacecraft and lowered it to the ground. We landed smoothly, and Joey flicked some switches. The spaceship's motors and computers slowly shut down. Joey was about to press the button to open the glass canopy, but I stopped him.

"Wait!" I said. "What if the air here isn't the same as it is on Earth? What if there isn't air here at all."

Joey thought a moment. "Okay," he said, "here's what we'll do. Take a deep breath and hold it. I'll open the canopy and breathe just a little. If something goes wrong, I'll close the canopy."

"That'll work," I said.

"Ready?" Joey asked, taking a deep breath. I took my own deep breath, then nodded.

"Here goes," he said, and suddenly, the canopy opened. Warm air (at least it *felt* like air) washed over us. Joey opened his mouth to breathe.

In and out. In and out. He looked like he was breathing fine.

I was just about to let out my breath, when suddenly, Joey started to gag. His hands grasped his neck. His eyes bulged, and a look of horror spread across his face.

Oh no! The air on 430-X wasn't air at all! It was *poison!*

21

I was horrified. Joey was gasping and choking, and I couldn't hold my breath much longer.

I reached across to try and press the lever to close the canopy, but I was still strapped to the seat by the belt that looped around my waist.

I wanted to scream, but I knew that if I did, then I would be breathing in the poisonous air, too.

And suddenly, just when I couldn't hold my breath any longer, Joey started laughing! He released his grasp on his neck. He laughed so hard that tears came to his eyes.

"Just kidding," he said.

"That was *not* funny!" I fumed, letting out my breath at the same time. I breathed deep. The air was warm and moist . . . similar to the air back on Earth.

"You should have seen your face!" Joey replied.

"Yeah, well, that wasn't a very nice thing to do," I snapped. "I really thought that you had breathed in poisonous air!"

"Check this place out," he said, ignoring me. "Look at those trees."

He pressed the button that released our seat belts, and we both climbed out of the craft and stood. It felt good after sitting in the same position for several million miles.

"Pink clouds," Joey said, looking up. "That's kind of bizarre."

"At least we know we can breathe," I replied. "That's a big relief."

Joey grabbed his neck and made gasping sounds again, and I poked him in the ribs.

"Okay, okay," he smirked. "Come on, Shelby. I was just kidding around."

"Well, quit it. We've got to find Arielle."

We climbed back into the spaceship. Joey closed the glass canopy and the craft roared to life.

"Let's head for that city, or whatever it is," I said.

The spaceship lifted off the ground. Soon, we were high in the sky.

"There it is, way over there," I said, pointing to what appeared to be structures on the horizon. "Head in that direction."

The craft was soon moving at an incredible speed. The green desert below us whirred past, and the structures in the distance became bigger, clearer. Joey slowed the craft as we neared the city.

"Look at that!" he cried, pointing.

Ahead of us, several spaceships flew up and around the city. A couple of them looked just like the one we were in. Some were bigger.

And the buildings were unbelievable. They appeared to be made of some sort of glassy stone. They shined in the sun, reflecting the bright glare.

"What if we're spotted?" I asked.

"As long as we have this spaceship," Joey replied, "we'll blend right in. I hope."

We kept going until we were on the outskirts of the city. More things came into view. I could see what appeared to be windows in some of the buildings. There were signs and billboards, too, just like we have on Earth, only the writing on the signs was nothing I could understand.

"Go down to the street," I said. "There's movement down there."

As you probably can imagine, this day was already the freakiest day in my life.

But it was about to get a lot freakier.

We were about to get our first look at an alien from 430-X.

22

Joey steered our spaceship down, in between giant buildings, down farther, approaching street level. Here, there were many other spaceships moving along, just a few feet off the ground. Some weren't moving at all, but rather, appeared to be parked.

And the aliens.

"Oh my gosh," I whispered quietly.

The beings were unlike anything I could have imagined. They were smaller than human adults, but they had three eyes! Their ears were large and long, and their noses were almost flat. None of the ones we saw had any hair. Their skin was a flat, olive color. And while they all appeared to have short legs, they moved very quickly. Without a doubt, they were the strangest looking creatures I had ever seen.

"I can't believe we're here," I breathed. *"Think about it, Joey. We're on another planet, millions of miles from Earth, looking at space aliens. No one on Earth has ever done this before."*

I was mesmerized by the things going on around us. We were in the middle of an alien city, and, if it weren't for the strange creatures walking about, and the spaceships in the air, the city would have been very similar to any city in the United States. I felt excited and scared at the same time.

"Let's not forget why we're here," Joey said. "We have to find Arielle."

"I don't have any idea where to start," I said. "I mean . . . she could be anywhere. And I don't think it would be really smart to walk up to one of these aliens and say something like *'hey . . . have you seen a girl Earthling with long hair wandering around anywhere?'"*

We were so caught up in watching what was going on around us that we didn't see the small group of aliens forming near a building.

Suddenly, we were surrounded by alien creatures! They came upon us so fast that there was nothing we could do. Their weird eyes—all three of them on each head—glared at us.

And all of them carried what appeared to be some sort of laser gun. They were making strange sounds, too, and appeared to be talking. I had no idea what they were saying, but I sure knew what they meant.

They wanted us out of the spacecraft . . . *now.*

23

We were in big trouble.

"*Can you try and take off?*" I whispered.

"*Yeah, but I don't like the looks of those guns they've got,*" Joey said. "*The last thing we need is to get blasted out of the sky.*"

The aliens were talking louder, urging us to get out of the craft. Reluctantly, Joey pressed the button and the glass canopy slid open.

Instantly, the aliens drew closer. They weren't pointing their laser guns at us anymore, and I was glad for that, but it was still a horrifying experience. One of the aliens grasped my arm and urged me out of the spaceship. Another one did the same to Joey. A few other aliens had gathered, peering curiously at us like we were from outer space.

Which, of course, we were. They had the same reaction to seeing us as we did when we saw them!

One of them was standing right in front of me. Its three big eyes glared at me, and it was chattering some sort of strange gibberish that I couldn't understand.

"I . . . I don't know what you're saying," I stammered. When I spoke, all of the other aliens stopped speaking. Joey was now beside me, which made me feel a little better. But we were both still very terrified.

They began talking among themselves, and it appeared like they were arguing. I glanced at Joey. He looked just as scared as I was.

Finally the six aliens motioned for us to walk, and we were led away. But they didn't put us in handcuffs or tie us up or anything, and I sure was glad about that!

Other aliens on the street were peering curiously at us as we walked past. I'm sure this was probably the first time they'd ever seen a human.

"Where do you think they're taking us?" I whispered.

"I don't have any idea," Joey whispered back.

Up ahead, a large spaceship came into view. It was very big . . . even bigger than some of the buildings we passed. The ship was oblong in shape, and appeared to be made of metal of some sort. Four enormous rocket thrusters jutted from one end, and there was a glass panel in front, that was, I presumed, the cockpit.

And it looked like that was where we were going to be taken.

"That thing is huge," I said as we walked toward the massive craft. Now I could see what appeared to be windows. The thing really did resemble something from a movie or television show.

A door opened downward, creating a stairway of sorts. When we reached it, the alien creatures urged us on. But we didn't walk, for the stairway was like an escalator, only flat. A track of some sort moved us along, and we were transported without any effort up to the waiting spaceship. In less than thirty seconds, we were inside, where we were greeted by still more aliens. They all looked at us curiously, like we were zoo animals.

One of the aliens came forward. He was holding what appeared to be two helmets in his hands. He handed one to Joey, who held it like he was holding fine china. Then the creature turned to me, said something in alien language, and placed the helmet on my head. It was sort of heavy.

After he placed it on my head, he urged Joey to do the same with the helmet he held. Reluctantly, Joey lifted the object up and placed it on his head.

The aliens were silent. All of them were looking at us, until one of the creatures began to speak—in English!

"Do you understand what I am saying?" the alien said. But here was the really weird part: his lips didn't match up with the words he was speaking! It was very strange.

"I . . . uh . . . yeah, I understand," I replied.

The creature looked at Joey. "Can you hear me?" he said.

Joey nodded, but he didn't speak.

"The helmet on your head is a computerized voice translator," the alien continued. "It is designed so that we may communicate with thousands of species from many different galaxies, including human beings."

I felt like I had a ball of yarn in my mouth. I still had all kinds of questions, but now I was so nervous that I couldn't speak. You would be, too, if you traveled through space only to be arrested by space aliens!

"I will begin by asking what it is that you are doing here," the alien said.

"We . . . we're looking for our friend," Joey replied. "We found a note that said she was kidnapped and taken here."

Joey's response caused the aliens to look at one another.

"And where did you get the spacecraft to travel here?" the alien asked.

"We found it on Earth," I replied. "It belonged to my teacher, Mrs. Rodriguez, who isn't a teacher at all. She's one of your androids."

Again, the aliens looked at one another.

"We know all about it," Joey said, getting braver. "We know all about your plans to invade Earth and steal all of our water."

"What have you done with Arielle?" I asked.

"We will not answer any of your questions," the alien replied. He looked at another alien. "Take them to a loading bay. Make certain that they do not leave."

Again, we were on the move. Two aliens marched us down a long, brightly-lit corridor. We were led into a small, empty room with no windows.

"Please give me the communicator helmets," one of the aliens said. Joey and I did what we were told.

"You will remain here," the other alien said, and without another word, he closed the door.

We were prisoners, all alone, on a planet millions of miles from Earth.

24

When the door closed and we were alone, I don't think I had ever felt so hopeless. There was nobody we could call, of course, and certainly no one to help us. We were the only humans for millions of miles.

Except, of course, for Arielle. She was somewhere on 430-X, but she had no idea that we had traveled here to try to rescue her. She was a prisoner, too . . . just like us.

"Man, we should have told someone about the aliens," Joey said, shaking his head. "Then we wouldn't be in this trouble."

"We tried, remember?" I replied with a shrug. "Nobody believed us. We did what we thought was right."

"There aren't even any windows we can try and climb through," I said. I looked up. "Not even an air vent."

Joey looked around, then he stood, walked to the door, and placed his ear against it.

"What are you doing?" I asked.

"Shhhh," Joey replied. "I'm listening."

He stood there for nearly a minute before he drew back. He looked at me and placed a finger on his lips. Then he reached down, grasped the doorknob, and turned it.

The door opened!

I let out a faint gasp and put my hand to my mouth. Once again, Joey placed a finger to his lips, urging me to be silent. He pushed the door open farther, then poked his head out, looking first to the right, then to the left. Then he turned and looked back at me, gesturing with his hand, urging me to come forward.

"None of them are around," he whispered. *"We've got to make a run for it."*

"What if we're spotted?" I whispered back.

"It's a chance we have to take. We don't have any other choice."

Joey was right. No one was coming to help us, and if we were going to escape, it was going to be completely up to us.

He tiptoed silently into the bright corridor, and I followed. Quickly, we headed back in the direction we had come from, stopping by an open door to make sure there were no aliens in the room to spot us. It was empty, and we continued on.

Soon, we came to a larger room filled with stacks and stacks of electrical equipment. It was the same place where we'd entered the spaceship.

But there was one problem.

Actually, there were *three* problems.

Aliens. Three of them. They were standing near something that looked like some sort of huge engine or motor. All three appeared to be working on it, and, at least for the moment, they were looking the other way.

Without a word, Joey pointed toward the open door of the craft. Beyond the door, I could see buildings and other aliens in the distance.

"Let's get out of here and see if we can find a spacecraft," Joey whispered.

"You . . . you mean steal *it?"* I replied.

"Exactly. We don't have any other options. Come on."

Before I knew it, Joey was tiptoeing across the room. We were in full view now, and if one of the aliens working on the engine turned, we would be spotted for sure.

But that's not what happened. We made it to the door and descended down the strange escalator. Thankfully, the only aliens we spotted were far off, and so far, we hadn't been noticed.

"Over there!" Joey said, pointing to an alien craft parked near a strange, dome-like structure. The dome was shiny and copper-colored, and I guessed that it might be a home of some sort.

We raced to the alien craft. It was very similar to the one we'd used to make our journey to 430-X, except it was wider. In seconds, we had slipped inside.

But there was a problem.

"I . . . I can't get this thing to fire up!" Joey said as he tried several buttons and switches. "It's different from the one we had!"

He tried several times to get the spaceship started, but nothing worked.

And now we had an even *bigger* problem.

An alien was coming out of the copper-colored dome . . . *and he was walking right toward the spacecraft that we were in!*

25

No matter what Joey tried, he couldn't get the spacecraft started.

And the alien was getting closer and closer by the second.

"Hurry!" I hissed. *"He's almost here!"*

"I'm trying!" Joey said. *"But it's no use! I can't get it going!"*

Just when I thought that the alien was going to reach down and open the glass canopy of the craft, he turned . . . and began walking back to the dome. Maybe he had forgotten something. Whatever the reason, it was a lucky break for us. My good luck charm sure paid off this time.

"We've got to get out of here and find another craft," Joey said. He pressed a button and the glass canopy rose up. In a flash, we leapt out and headed around to the other side of the copper-colored dome. Here, we were able to hunker down without being seen—at least for the moment.

We watched as the alien returned to his craft, climbed inside, and started it up. The motor made a soft, electrical hum, then rose up into the air. In seconds, it had vanished.

"That was a close one," I said with a sigh of relief.

"Yeah, too close," Joey agreed. "But we have to find another craft."

"How about the one that we came in?" I suggested.

Joey shook his head. "That would be best," he said, "but it's too far away. We'd be spotted for sure. Besides . . . the aliens might have taken it somewhere. We're going to have to find one that's closer."

"But what if we have the same problem?" I asked. "What if we can't get it started?"

Joey didn't say anything. We both knew what we had to do . . . we had to find an alien craft and make it back to Earth. From there, I didn't know exactly what we'd do, but when people saw us flying around in an alien spaceship, they'd have to believe us for sure!

"Let's sneak around the side of the dome and see if there are any other spaceships around," Joey said.

We ducked down and slipped around behind the dome. In the distance, we could see the large spaceship where we'd been taken. I knew that it was only a matter of time before the aliens had discovered that we'd escaped. It would be lot harder to find a spacecraft and slip away if we had a bunch of galactic freaks chasing us.

"Look over there," I said, pointing to several spaceships hovering near a building in the distance. As we watched, one or two of the crafts would leave, and two more would descend from the sky. We watched aliens get out and attend to their parked craft.

Suddenly, Joey's eyes lit up. "You know what that is?!?!" he exclaimed. "It's an alien gas station! I'll bet that's where they're refueling!"

The longer I watched, the more I realized that Joey was right. It was just like a gas station on Earth. When an alien was finished refueling the craft, he walked into the building and returned moments later, climbed into the craft, and sped upward into the sky.

"Let's go," Joey said. "That's going to be our best chance yet."

"But there are aliens all around," I said. "We'll never make it without being seen."

"It doesn't matter," Joey said. "All we have to do is act fast. I'm sure we'll be spotted . . . but if we can get a head start, I don't think they'll be able to catch us."

Was the plan crazy? Yes. Insane? That, too.

But at least it was a plan . . . and like it or not, we were going through with it.

It would all be a matter of who was faster: the aliens . . . or us.

26

While we watched from a distance, we saw a craft land near what could only have been the fuel pumps.

"There's one," Joey said. "It's good-sized, too. Bigger than the one we piloted from Earth. Let's wait for the alien to fill up and go inside."

I clasped my good luck charm that dangled around my neck. So far, it had worked pretty good. Sure, we'd had some pretty rotten luck when we had been captured by the aliens . . . but we had pretty good luck when we escaped. We had bad luck when Joey couldn't get the spacecraft started a few minutes ago; we had good luck when we were able to get out of the craft and escape when the alien was coming.

For a good luck charm, it wasn't working all that bad. I just hoped that our luck would continue, especially since we were millions of miles from home.

"There he goes," Joey said. "Let's go for it!"

We sprang from our hiding place at the side of the building and sprinted toward the waiting spaceship. I didn't look at anything else except our destination, as I didn't want to be distracted by a single thing. The only thing I concentrated on was running . . . and *fast*.

Joey is a better runner than I am, and he reached the craft first. The glass canopy was open, and he dove inside.

"What luck!" he exclaimed. "It's still running!"

I reached the space vehicle and climbed in. It was bigger than Mrs. Rodriguez's craft, with two passenger seats behind us. "Let's get out of here!" I said, panting and out of breath.

Joey pressed a button on the control panel, and the glass canopy lowered and locked into place. He was able to figure out the small craft's navigation system rather quickly, and in the next instant, the craft was rising up.

"We've got company again," I said, pointing toward the building.

The alien was returning to his spaceship. When he saw his own space vehicle rising into the air, all three of his eyes doubled in size!

But worst of all, the alien wasted no time in grasping his laser gun that was strapped to his waist.

"Let's get out of here!" I exclaimed.

Suddenly, a blinding quill of yellow light shot past us. Then another.

"He's shooting at us, Joey!" I screamed. *"Get this thing moving!"*

The craft rocketed upward so suddenly that I thought I was going to have to pull my tongue out of my stomach! It felt like a giant hand was pushing me against the seat.

Another needle of yellow went zinging past, and I knew that if we didn't get out of range soon, we were going to be blown to bits.

"Faster, Joey, faster!" I cried, even though I knew that we were already going about as fast as we could. I just *really* wanted to get out of there, pronto!

But Joey knew just what to do. The craft spiraled around, spinning through the sky like a spear. Within seconds, the alien city below us was only a speck. The yellow laser bolts no longer threatened, and soon, the sky above went from blue to deep blue, darker still, until stars began to appear.

I grasped my good luck charm. It was really working, after all. We were going to make it back to Earth.

"Uh oh," Joey said, and I could feel the spacecraft begin to slow.

"What is it?" I asked. "What's wrong?"

"Up ahead," Joey replied. "Look."

I peered into dark space. Billions of stars dotted a black curtain.

"What?" I repeated. "What do you see?"

"The same thing we saw coming in," Joey said.

I strained to see what he was seeing. Suddenly, shapes came into view.

My heart sank.

My blood ran cold.

Ahead of us . . . directly in front of us . . . was the line of alien warships.

And they were facing our direction.

27

The terror I felt at that moment was overwhelming.

In front of us was an army of warships . . . and they were all facing our direction.

Maybe my good luck charm wasn't bringing such good luck, after all.

"What are we going to do?" I asked.

Joey didn't respond right away. He allowed our ship to drift quietly. I think he was trying to come up with a plan. His eyes scanned the control panel, the floor, and then, finally, the line of alien warships that were suspended in space, ready to strike.

"I think we can get away," he said.

"What?!?! How?!?!" I exclaimed.

"Take a look around this spaceship," he replied. "This isn't an ordinary space vehicle."

"And since when did you know so much about space vehicles?" I said. "You drove one for the first time only a few hours ago."

"But look, Shelby. Look at all of this equipment on the outside of our craft. Look at these levers. Take a look at those cannons right beneath the canopy. We have our own warship. That's what this thing is, Shelby! A small warship. Like a small starfighter."

"But Joey! There's got to be fifty warships ahead of us! We can't fight all of them!"

"No, but we might be able to outmaneuver them," Joey replied. "We're smaller, so we have that advantage."

"Not if they start shooting right now," I said.

"I don't think they can fire right now," Joey mused. His gaze never left the line of looming warships ahead of us. "See . . . we're right in line with 430-X. If they fire a laser shot—or anything else, for that matter—and miss, there's a chance it will continue on and hit the city on 430-X. They're going to wait until there isn't any danger of a stray shot hitting their planet."

"So what do we do?" I asked. "As soon as they have a clear shot, they're going to blast us to smithereens."

"They'll try," Joey said. "But maybe we can be gone before that happens."

"How?"

"We'll keep drifting slowly in their direction. I'll program the onboard navigational system to head back to Earth. If I time it right, we can warp to light speed before they have time to shoot. Once we do that, we'll be going too fast for them to fire at us."

"Can't they travel as fast as we can?" I asked.

Joey shrugged. "Probably. But if we have a head start, we just might be able to make it back to Earth before they do. And they probably don't want to go to our planet just yet, because they're not quite ready to invade. They're probably awaiting word from Mrs. Rodriguez . . . which will probably come soon. But if Mrs. Rodriguez discovers her spacecraft is missing, she might put off the invasion. At least for the moment."

I sighed heavily. "I hope you're right," I said quietly.

Ahead of us, the line of warships waited. Each craft was massive, and I could see the barrels of their laser cannons pointed at us.

"Make sure you're buckled in tight," Joey said as he fiddled with the computer keypad on the control panel. On the screen, rows and rows of numbers and letters flashed.

"There," Joey replied. "Earth." He tapped at the keypad, then looked up at the warships ahead of us. "Are you ready?"

"I guess so," I said. But I didn't sound very convincing. After all . . . how could you ever be ready for something like this?

"I'm going to head right beneath them," Joey said. "Then I'll engage the navigating system, and we'll hit light speed."

I didn't say anything. I reached up and touched my good luck charm, glad that it was still there. I sure hope that it still worked!

"Here we go," Joey said. "Get ready."

Suddenly, our craft made an explosive dive. The line of warships ahead of us were now above us. Joey flipped a switch on the control panel, but nothing happened. We were going fast, but certainly not light speed.

A laser blast suddenly rocketed past, followed immediately by another one. Both of the shots were so close that they rocked our small spacecraft. I turned and looked up, and was horrified to see more lasers being fired.

"Joey, we've got to get out of here!" I shrieked.

"We are! Hang on!"

A laser blast suddenly went sailing by us, followed by two more, and another.

Without warning, I was pushed back into my seat. Once again, I had that feeling of being pressed back, like there was a heavy brick on my chest. The stars around us turned into white streaks. Our spaceship shook and shuddered as we rocketed through space.

"We're on our way!" Joey shouted.

The roar of the craft's rockets was almost deafening. I tried to imagine what we looked like, headed through space at such a speed. There was probably a plume of fire a half mile long behind us!

And there was something else behind us, too. Something we couldn't see.

But when our spaceship was rocked by a sudden explosion, it became all too clear what was going on.

There was a warship behind us.

Our tiny spaceship was suddenly spinning, whirling madly out of control, knocked off course, flailing through space.

28

I felt like I was on a tilt-a-whirl at the fair, only going a hundred times faster.

Warning lights were flashing, and sirens were screaming. I was so dizzy that I felt faint. My good luck charm was still around my neck, but it was flying all about, hitting my face and shoulders.

Some good luck charm it turned out to be!

The sirens stopped chirping, and some of the warning lights blinked out. I felt the ship begin to steady. Gradually, Joey was able to bring the craft under control.

Which was a relief—but not very much. We hadn't been hurt, but I knew now that our situation was grim.

"The laser blast didn't hit us," Joey said, "but it came so close that it knocked out our rockets."

"You mean . . . we don't have any power?" I asked.

"Nothing," Joey said somberly. He tried a few controls on the panel, but nothing worked. "We have power, but we don't have our engines. And without our engines, we'll eventually run out of power. Plus, we've been knocked out of light speed. At the speed we're going, it'll take us ten thousand years to get back to Earth."

"Ten thousand years!?!?" I exclaimed.

But there really wasn't anything we could do. About the only good news was the fact that there were no longer any alien warships in pursuit. They probably thought that they'd hit us, and we weren't going to pose any more threat to them . . . which was pretty much true. Now that we didn't have control over our spacecraft, there wasn't anything we could do to stop the alien invasion.

"So, now what do we do?" I asked.

Joey sighed, then he looked at me. "I don't think there's anything we *can* do," he replied. "I can't get the motor started, and I don't know much about fixing rocket engines. I can steer, but that's not going to help us get back to Earth. There's not much we can do."

Well, Joey was wrong about that. There was absolutely *nothing* we could do. There was no one we could call or radio, and no one was going to rescue us. The only thing we could do was watch the stars as our spacecraft descended deeper and deeper into space.

We didn't speak for a long time. Soon, I grew tired and closed my eyes. I tried hard not to cry, but I did just a tiny bit.

Soon, I fell asleep.

When I awoke I was confused, and it took me a moment to realize where I was. When I did, my sorrow and grief was as heavy as a truck.

Joey was sleeping in the seat next to me, snoring softly. I had no watch, so I had no idea how long we'd been dozing.

A sudden movement caught my eye, and I looked up and gazed out the glass canopy.

I gasped.

I rubbed my eyes.

I gasped again.

My eyes just about fell out of my head.

I grasped Joey's leg and shook him. *"Joey!"* I cried. *"Wake up! You've got to see this!"*

29

Joey jolted awake. I could tell that he, too, was a little confused. But when he saw the scene in front of us, he gasped. His jaw hung down, but he was speechless.

In front of the craft we could see what only could be some sort of space station. There were three large, dome-shaped units, similar to the copper-colored dome we'd seen on 430-X. Only these domes were bright white, nearly blinding.

But perhaps what was most amazing were the other spaceships that whirled around it. There were perhaps a half dozen vessels about the size of ours. Several were hovering in space nearby, while a few were parked near the domes. While we watched, large doors would open up in the domes and allow several spaceships to enter or leave. Then the doors would close.

"What do you think it is?" I asked.

Joey shook his head slowly. "Some sort of space port," he replied.

While we watched, more spaceships came and went. I was afraid that we might be spotted by one of the aliens from 430-X, but so far, nobody seemed to be paying any attention to us.

And as our craft drifted closer and closer to the strange station suspended in space, something else came into view.

"Look," I said, pointing.

Coming into view was what could only be described as a billboard. It was a giant sign with a picture of some alien creature on the left. To the right of the alien were words in plain English. They read:

BIG LOU'S INTERPLANETARY
SPACE STATION & DELI
snacks - fuel - spaceship repairs (minor and major)

"I don't believe I'm seeing this," Joey said. "At any moment I'm going to wake up and all of this will be just a dream."

"I wish that's what it was," I said. "But it's real. The only thing I want to know is why that sign is made in English. You would think that it would be created in some other alien language."

Joey's eyes widened. "Maybe there are English speaking aliens there!" he said. "There might even be real human beings!"

134

Hope grew. Here we were, in the middle of outer space. Our spacecraft was damaged, and we had no way to return to Earth.

But now we were fortunate enough to drift right to an interplanetary space station. Whoever Big Lou was, the billboard hanging in space said that his store fixes spaceships.

"Let's maneuver down there," I said. "Do you think we can do it without the engine?"

"I have a little control of the craft," Joey said, taking the steering levers into his hand. "We don't have any power, but it shouldn't be too difficult. I'll try and take us in and land on the platform near that silver spaceship."

Joey carefully steered the craft toward the space station. Other crafts were leaving and arriving. Big Lou's was a pretty popular place.

As soon as we neared the station, a door opened in the dome. A strange alien was standing in the entry way, waving us in. He had human features, but his head seemed much larger than his body. He had no hair at all, and his skin was a sandy brown color with a waxy appearance. And he was wearing a gray suit. Some sort of breathing apparatus was over his mouth, and a tube hung down over what I presumed was his chest. The tube twisted and went back over his shoulder.

Joey gently nudged the craft inside, and the door slid silently closed behind us.

We were in a garage of some sorts. There were several spaceships parked next to one another. Strange tools lay on the floor and on a few work tables that lined the walls. There were no doors or windows, or any other aliens that we could see.

And I have to admit, I was a little afraid of what we were getting ourselves into. After all, the aliens on 430-X didn't like us one bit. What if there were other aliens here that felt the same way?

Regardless, we didn't have any choice. Our only other option would be to drift into space until—

I couldn't bear to think about it.

The strange creature with the big head removed his breathing apparatus and began speaking gibberish to us. At least, it sure *sounded* like gibberish. I certainly couldn't understand a word of what he was saying.

"I think he wants us to raise the canopy," Joey said. He pressed a button, and the canopy rose up.

The alien continued speaking, and it looked like he was getting frustrated. When he got a closer look at the two of us seated in the spacecraft, he threw up his hands, walked to a table—

—and picked up a laser gun!

30

My heart skipped a beat, and a lump grew in my throat. My eyes darted around for somewhere to run, but the only door I saw was on the other side of the garage . . . and we'd have to get past the alien to get there.

As it turned out, however, there was no reason to run. The alien had picked up the laser gun, all right, but only to move it out of the way. He set it down at the end of the table and picked up two helmets: the exact kind of helmets we were given on 430-X so we could communicate with the aliens. He walked to us and handed us the headgear.

After placing them on our heads, we could understand what he was saying. It seemed he was speaking perfect English, but his mouth didn't match his speech. It was weird.

"I don't understand why creatures simply don't carry their communication helmets with them at all times," he was saying. "You'll never make it around space that way. Now . . . what is it that you need?"

"Well, our spacecraft has been damaged," Joey said. "We need someone to fix it."

"What's wrong with it?" the alien said, getting right to the point.

"Well, we were being shot at," Joey began. "We didn't get hit, I don't think. But the laser blast came very close."

The alien knelt down and inspected the large round thrusters that jutted out the back of our craft.

"Uh-huh," he said, running a wiry hand over the thruster. "Electrical demogrification of the atomic cylinder."

"Yeah, that's what I was thinking," Joey said, rolling his eyes as he looked at me. I snickered, and it felt good. There hadn't been much to laugh at lately.

"What's that mean?" I asked the alien.

He stood up and turned around, and I could see once again how large his head was compared to his body. His eyes were quite large, too, but they were very, very dark, like the deep, glossy eyes of a chipmunk. "It means that it is repairable, but it will take some time. You may wish to browse the store while you're waiting."

That sounded like a good idea, but I was still a little nervous.

"Say, Mister . . . um, alien-dude," I began.

"I am Quantar," the alien said with a slight bow. "I am the head mechanic here."

"Yeah, okay," I said. "But . . . we're not from around here. Just what is this place?"

Quantar looked at me like I was from outer space, which, in fact, I was.

"I mean," I continued, "is this sort of like a gas station?"

Quantar frowned, and his entire, massive forehead wrinkled. "While I am not familiar with your term 'gas station'," he said, "Big Lou's is a full service spacecraft convenience store. Aliens from many galaxies stop here for food, fuel for their spaceships, things like that. They come here for the same reason you did."

"But we're kind of in a lot of trouble," Joey said. "You see, the aliens of planet 430-X want to invade our planet and steal all of our water."

"430-X?!?!" Quantar exclaimed. "Why those nasty creatures! That's all those Xers do. Cause trouble in the galaxy."

"Xers?" I quizzed.

"That's short for 'Xanthyicariumnipnoidupalys'," Quantar explained. "That's their technical name. We just call them Xers for short. Why, sometimes, we don't even allow them in the store! But the Raeoleans have been tracking them and trying to stop them."

Xers? I thought. *Raeoleans? How many races of space aliens are there?*

But Quantar's reply answered my next question. I had been afraid that there might be aliens from planet 430-X in the store, but from what Quantar was saying, it wasn't likely . . . and that was a good thing.

"What about that sign out there?" I asked. "How is it that it's printed in our language, when we have to wear these helmets to translate?"

"The board is equipped with brain wave sensors," Quantar replied. "When you get close to it, the computer chips in the sign automatically sense your brain waves, and create a message that is crafted in your native language. Otherwise, we'd have to have thousands of signs . . . one for each different language that aliens speak. You two aren't from around here, are you?"

"We're from a place called Earth," I said. "And that's where we'd like to get back to."

"Well, I'll do the best I can with your ship. Go on, go on," Quantar urged. "Go look around in the store. You might even see something you want. I'll come and get you when your craft is fixed."

Quantar made a motion to the closed door on the other side of the space garage. I looked at Joey, and he looked at me. He shrugged. "Might as well," he said, and we walked across the cluttered garage to the door that opened into the store.

Now, we'd had some bizarre things happen to us since we'd stolen Mrs. Rodriguez's spaceship . . . but it was nothing compared to what we saw when we went through those doors and into Big Lou's store.

31

Halloween.

It's the only thing that came to mind. Looking at all of the different aliens that filled Big Lou's store was like a costume party.

There were tall aliens, thin ones, aliens with tiny heads, big heads. Aliens with six eyes, aliens with three legs. One alien had two heads, and they were arguing with one another. Music was playing from somewhere.

There were several aisles of groceries, and Joey and I walked among them, inspecting the goods. Much of what we found was a lot like what you'd find at a grocery store on Earth: snacks, canned goods, bottles containing liquids which looked like they might be the alien equivalent of soda pop. Aliens walked around us, talking to one another. They didn't seem to pay any attention to us.

"It would be cool to take something back to Earth," I said. "Can you imagine taking alien macaroni and cheese into show and tell?"

Joey laughed. "I don't have any money," he said, "or I'd get something."

"I don't, either," I said.

Suddenly, I had a horrifying thought. "Joey!" I exclaimed. "If we don't have any money, how are we going to pay for the repairs to the spacecraft?!?!"

Joey's eyes got huge. He hadn't thought of that, either.

"Let's wander around and try to come up with something," he said. "I don't even know what they use for money around here."

"Maybe we can sweep the floor to earn some money," I said. "I've done that at my uncle's store."

"I don't know what the repairs are going to cost," Joey said, "but I don't think we'll be able to earn enough money by sweeping floors."

And soon . . . all too soon, as a matter of fact, Quantar found us in the store.

"You're all set," he said to us. "Good as new." Then he handed Joey a piece of paper.

A bill.

"How . . . how much do we owe you?" Joey said as he inspected the bill. I looked at it, but it was written, of course, in alien language. It looked like a bunch of scribbles.

"Five hundred thousand kerkars," the alien said.

"Well . . . um . . . we . . . we have a problem," Joey stammered. "We, uh . . . we don't have any kerkars, whatever they are."

Quantar's glossy black eyes shimmered. "What?" he said. "No kerkars? How do you expect to pay for the work done to your spacecraft?" He glared at us, and I was liking this less and less as the seconds ticked past.

Joey looked at me pleadingly, but my eyes had no answer for him. I was frantically trying to think of something. Maybe if we were nice to Quantar and explained our situation, he would let us go without paying.

But I doubted it.

Suddenly, a flare lit up in Joey's eyes. He looked at Quantar, then back to me. "I think we can come up with a solution," he said. He turned to face the alien. "Do you mind if I speak with my friend alone?" he asked. "We aren't going anywhere, I promise."

Quantar nodded warily. Joey took me by the hand and led me around an aisle where a large, purple alien with seven eyes was mulling over what appeared to be a box of cereal.

"What's your plan?" I asked him.

"It's perfect!" he hissed, and when he explained his idea, I told him that he had lost his mind, that he was crazy—but I also had to admit, it was a good idea . . . and it just might work.

32

We walked back up to Quantar. "Okay," I said, "here's what we're going to do. Shelby, give me your gold jewel." He pointed at the cheap plastic ring I was wearing on the chain around my neck. My 'good luck charm' was now an expensive piece of jewelry.

At least, that's what we were hoping that Quantar would believe.

I slipped the necklace off and handed it to Joey.

"Quantar, this is very valuable. We'll give it to you in trade for the work on our spacecraft."

"No way!" I protested loudly. "It's worth a lot of kerkars! Twice as much as what the repairs cost!"

Quantar watched with curious, scrutinizing eyes.

"Shelby," Joey said, "we don't have any other way to pay for the repairs. We have no kerkars, nothing."

"What is this 'gold' that you speak of?" Quantar asked, eyeing the plastic gold ring in my hand.

"It's a rare piece of jewelry," I said. "As a matter of fact, you probably can search for a zillion miles around, and not find anything like it."

Quantar reached out and picked up the ring with a thin hand. He rolled it around, inspecting it with a peculiar, scornful gaze.

"Of course, we'd need to have more for it than just the repairs, because it is so rare, Joey said."

"How much is this worth?" Quantar asked.

"Why, you might find someone willing to pay you over a million kerkars," Joey replied. "Like I said . . . it's very, very rare."

"Joey!" I cried. "We can't trade that! It's too valuable!"

Joey looked at me. "Shelby, we have to. Quantar, can we talk for a moment? Alone?"

Quantar looked at him, then at me. "This way," he said, motioning Joey to follow him. Joey mouthed the words 'don't worry' to me. I tried not to worry, but it was hard.

They walked over to the other side of an aisle. I couldn't hear what was being said, but I could tell that Joey was doing everything he could to persuade Quantar to accept the plastic ring as trade for his services. Then Joey followed Quantar through the door that led to the garage, and disappeared.

After a few minutes, Joey returned . . . with a big smile on his face.

"Well?" I asked hopefully.

Joey's grin widened. "It worked! I was able to trade him your ring for the repair work!"

"I hope he never gets to Earth and finds out that its only cheap plastic," I said.

"Hey, you never know. Because we're from Earth, that would make the ring very rare. And it very well could be valuable on this side of the galaxy. Come on. Let's get out of here."

I followed Joey through the door and into the garage. Just before the door closed behind me, I took one last look at the strange scene in Big Lou's, and a thought came to me.

Even if I did have a camera and was able to take pictures, people still wouldn't believe me, I thought. *They'd think that I took pictures at a costume party.*

I turned and walked into the garage. Quantar was hustling around, putting things away and organizing the garage.

"We've got another ship coming in," he said, "so you two will have to be on your way."

"Thanks for everything," I said, and I lifted the communication helmet from my head and handed it to him. He said something back to me, but without my helmet I couldn't understand him. I'm sure, however, that he was saying goodbye, so I nodded and did the same.

Joey removed his helmet as well, and handed it to Quantar. Then we climbed into the spacecraft.

"We've got to hurry," Joey said as the glass canopy came down. The automatic seat belts fastened themselves. Joey made some adjustments on the control panel.

"Here goes," he said.

Suddenly, the rocket boosters behind us rumbled. At that moment, I didn't think I'd heard a sweeter sound in my life.

Quantar opened the door behind us. Joey piloted the craft, raising it off the floor a few inches. Then he carefully guided it back, onto the platform. Another alien craft was waiting to enter, so we continued backing up until we were far enough away to rise up.

"What luck," Joey said as our craft rose high above the interplanetary space station.

"Yeah, thanks to that good luck charm you gave me," I said.

Joey worked at the control panel, fiddling with the computer navigation. Finally, he was ready.

"Next stop: Earth," he said. "You ready?"

"I was ready a long time ago," I replied.

"Hang on then," he said.

Suddenly, we were moving forward very fast, faster, faster still, until all of the stars turned into lines.

"Light speed," Joey said.

We were finally on our way. We were going back to Earth. Whatever happened from now on . . . well, we'd have to wait and see.

And now that we had proof, we could confront Mrs. Rodriguez. Perhaps she knew where Arielle had been taken.

But another thought kept creeping into my mind.

What if we're already too late?

33

It didn't take very long to make it back to Earth. After all, when you're traveling faster than the speed of light, it doesn't take you very long to go *anywhere*. The ship began to slow, and a dot far, far in the distance began to grow larger.

Earth. Home.

"I've programmed the navigational system to take us right back to the warehouse where Mrs. Rodriguez's spaceship was stored," Joey said. "That way, we'll have a place where we can leave this thing without anyone finding out about it."

"But if we show it to people, they'd have to believe us," I said.

Joey shook his head. "We can do that later. Right now, we've got to find a way to stop the androids and the aliens."

"But how?" I asked. It seemed like an impossible task for two kids and a single spaceship.

"I have an idea," Joey replied, "but I can't tell you yet."

We were getting closer and closer to Earth. From space, the planet sure looked cool. It was blue and white, and I could see all of North America, surrounded by oceans.

"Hang on," Joey said. "It's going to be bumpy as we enter Earth's atmosphere."

The craft began to shake and rock, but not too bad. After two minutes, the trembling eased. The atmosphere around us gradually went from black to dark blue, then light blue. Beneath us was the entire United States. It was so cool, looking at it from so high up!

Down we plunged, heading toward the ground. The more we dropped, the less we could see of the entire country. Soon, I could make out the city of Scottsdale. Buildings and streets began to appear.

"I hope nobody sees us," I said. "We'll have a hard time explaining how two kids swiped a spaceship from a planet millions of miles away."

"We'll go straight to the warehouse," Joey said, "and I'll guide the craft inside. Once we're inside, you get out and close the big garage door. Hopefully, we can make it inside without anyone noticing."

I was amazed at how fast we were going, but Joey had learned to be a pretty good pilot. He slowed as we neared the city, and then he zipped the spacecraft down to street level, winding around the warehouse to the garage door. I looked around to see if there was anyone watching, but I didn't see anybody.

Joey guided the craft through the garage door, and then lowered us to the floor. As soon as we touched down he cut the engines, and the droning sound of the rocket boosters began to diminish. The glass canopy raised and I leapt out and raced to the garage door. I pressed a button on the wall and the large door began to roll down.

"Perfect," I said to Joey, who was climbing out of the spacecraft. "Now we can pay a visit to Mrs. Rodriguez."

"I don't think that will be necessary," said a voice from not far away.

Mrs. Rodriguez!

While we watched, she appeared from behind a large pile of crates.

"That won't be necessary at all," she repeated as she walked toward us. "I think it's time we put a stop to your shenanigans . . . *once and for all.*"

34

Mrs. Rodriguez walked calmly, cooly, toward us. She looked like she meant *business*. Before, I had always been afraid of Mrs. Rodriguez because she gave me too much homework.

Now I had an entirely *different* reason to fear her.

"You thought you would outsmart me, didn't you?" she hissed. "Well, you're a little late. Matter of fact, you're a *lot* late. Far too late to stop us."

And with that, Mrs. Rodriguez did something totally unexpected: she reached up and placed both hands over her face, as if she was crying, hiding her emotions. But in the next instant her face was in her hands . . . and I mean *in her hands! Mrs. Rodriguez had removed her face!*

Now, her true self—what she really was—was exposed. Her features were no longer human. Now, a tangle of wires and electronics were exposed, making her look like a horrifying robot. There were dark lenses where her eyes had been, and I imagined that they were probably some sort of cameras that allowed the android to 'see' just like a human.

"You'll never get away with this," Joey said as he stood next to the spacecraft. "We know everything. We've even been to 430-X."

"I know all about your misadventures," the android snapped. "You were very lucky to escape, and even luckier to be able to evade the alien patrols. But now, it is time to end this silly game. The aliens from 430-X will invade, and there is nothing that two children are going to do to stop them."

"You'll have to stop us first," Joey said, and he swung his leg up and stepped into the spacecraft. At first, I thought he was going to try and take off, and I almost ran up and jumped into the spaceship.

But that's not what Joey did. He reached down into the cockpit . . . and pulled out a laser gun!

"You're foolish," the android snapped. "You don't know what you're doing."

"I know exactly what I'm doing," Joey said, training the laser gun on the android.

"And I do, too," another voice said.

Upon hearing the voice, we turned. The voice was familiar, but there was no one to see.

Then we heard footsteps echoing in the building, and when I saw who was emerging from behind a stack of crates, my jaw fell. I gasped.

Arielle! Arielle was walking toward us, carrying a laser gun!

"Arielle!" I shouted. "I am so glad to see you! We thought we'd never see you again!"

"I'm glad to see you, too," she said . . . and with that, she aimed her laser gun right toward us!

35

"Arielle!" I shouted. "What are you doing?!?!"

"What do you think she's doing?" Mrs. Rodriguez replied. "She's an android . . . just like me."

"That's right," Arielle said, and with one hand she peeled away the human mask that covered her face.

I gasped. So did Joey.

"Drop your laser gun, Joey," Arielle ordered. Joey knelt down and placed the laser gun on the cement floor.

"Kick it over here."

Joey did as he was asked. The laser gun skittered across the floor, and Mrs. Rodriguez picked it up.

"But . . . but why?" I asked Arielle. I was dumbfounded. I'd believed all along that Arielle was my friend. After all . . . I've known her more than a year!

"I was sent to the school to make sure that no one discovered our plans," she said. "You see, there was always

159

a chance that someone might find out. When you became suspicious, I had to act."

"But why fake your own kidnapping?" Joey asked. "That doesn't make sense."

"Sure it does," Mrs. Rodriguez replied. "When we thought you were getting too close to finding out about the plan, we decided that the best way to get you both out of the picture was to lure you to 430-X, by using my spacecraft. I was here the whole time, watching both of you. I didn't stop you because I wanted you to take the ship. I wanted you to go to 430-X."

"But you didn't plan on us coming back," I said.

"No, we didn't. But it doesn't matter anymore. The aliens from 430-X are preparing for the invasion. However, to make sure you two don't interfere any more than you already have, we'll be taking you with us to the secret base. You should feel very lucky—you both have a front row seat for the invasion. Now—both of you—get in the back seat of the spacecraft. We're going for a little ride."

"Somebody will see the spaceship," I said. "You'll never get out of the city without someone seeing you."

Although her face was that of a robot, Mrs. Rodriguez could still smile. She looked eerie. "You are a very silly girl," she said. "It doesn't matter anymore. Everything is in its place. No one can stop us now."

Reluctantly, Joey and I climbed into the back of the craft.

Arielle the android walked over to the large garage door and pressed the 'open' button. The door began to roll up, and Arielle turned and walked to the spacecraft where Mrs. Rodriguez had already taken her seat in front of us.

I thought about trying to fight them off and take over the spacecraft, but I didn't think we'd succeed. After all . . . Arielle and Mrs. Rodriguez weren't human . . . they were androids. They probably have super-human strength.

"Where are you taking us?" Joey asked.

"To the place where we've secretly built the alien's headquarters on Earth," Mrs. Rodriguez replied. The spacecraft began to rise into the air. "To the Grand Canyon. It's the only place big enough to build a headquarters that the aliens will need. Of course, once the water is compressed and taken back to 430-X, there will be no need for a base . . . or humans, for that matter."

The spacecraft drifted out of the building. As soon as we cleared the garage door we rocketed up into the sky at an incredible speed, racing over the city and traveling still higher yet.

Within minutes we approached the Grand Canyon, which seemed incredible. Usually, it's a four and a half hour drive from Scottsdale to the Grand Canyon, but at the speed we were traveling, it only took us a few minutes!

Mrs. Rodriguez steered the craft down, down, deeper still, into the massive expanse of jagged, colorful rock formations. Near the floor of the canyon the craft slowed, carefully maneuvering between rock formations. However, as we touched down, I realized that the formations here on the canyon floor weren't made of rock at all! They were buildings, with their roofs cleverly disguised as rock! From above, they didn't look like buildings at all.

A few people scurried about, but I wasn't fooled. I knew that they weren't humans . . . they were androids. The arrival of our craft went seemingly unnoticed by the other androids who were busy making final preparations for the invasion.

The glass canopy of our spacecraft opened, and hot, dry air enveloped us.

"Out," Mrs. Rodriguez the android ordered, and Joey and I climbed out of the craft. Arielle still held her laser gun, but she wasn't pointing it at us.

"Where do you want them?" she asked Mrs. Rodriguez.

"In an empty storage room," Mrs. Rodriguez answered. "And make sure they can't escape. Not that it would matter now, but just in case."

Arielle motioned us toward a small building, and I caught the look on Joey's face.

He was *smiling*.

Oh, it wasn't *much* of a smile. Just a slight crick at the corner of each side of his mouth.

But he was definitely smiling.

We approached the building. It was made of wood and metal, but it was painted to match the colors of the rock and sediment of the canyon walls and floor. The door was also painted, and until we were right in front of it, I didn't even know it was there.

From behind us, Arielle spoke coldly. "Open it," Arielle said.

162

I reached out and grasped the knob. It, too, was painted like the walls, and was nearly invisible.

The door opened into an empty, stark white room. There were three glass windows without any curtains or blinds. Sunshine streamed through, giving the room a yellow, sulphur-like appearance.

"Inside," was all Arielle said, and we obeyed. The door closed behind us, and I heard it lock. We weren't going *anywhere.*

I looked at Joey, and his smile widened. His grin stretched temple-to-temple, and his eyes lit up.

"It's time you found out something about me," he said.

Now, I had thought that what had happened to us so far was pretty incredible. Fantastic, even. I mean . . . in one day, we'd discovered a spacecraft, traveled faster than the speed of light to another planet, had been captured by aliens, escaped, only to be captured again. I don't know about *you,* but things like that don't happen to *me* every day.

But I was totally blown away by what Joey did next.

36

Just like I had watched Mrs. Rodriguez and Arielle do earlier, Joey reached up and placed his hands over his face . . . *and pulled away his mask!*

Talk about being horrified! All along, I had thought Joey was my friend . . . only to discover that he, too, was an android!

I leapt away from him and backed against a wall.

"Stay away from me!" I shrieked.

Joey slipped his mask back on. "Hey, take it easy. I've got some explaining to do. When you hear what I have to say, you'll understand. But first, I need to do something, and you might think it's a little strange."

"Too late for that," I said. "Everything I've seen today is more than just a little strange. It's a *lot* strange."

While I watched, Joey raised his arm . . . and pulled away a large piece of skin!

At least, that's what it looked like at first. But I soon realized that it wasn't skin . . . it was a panel of some sort. When he pulled it back, I could see a few buttons and wires—even tiny blinking lights—inside his arm!

"Don't worry," Joey explained while he fiddled with the electronics in his arm. "You'll understand everything in a moment. But first, I need to send a signal to alert the Raeoleans to our whereabouts."

Wait a minute, I thought. *Raeoleans? Isn't that the race of aliens that have been trying to track the aliens from 430-X?*

Joey was busy tapping some small keys that were in his arm. When he finished, he replaced the 'skin', smiled, and looked at me.

"Yes," he began, "I, too, am an android. However, I was created and sent here by the Raeoleans. They have been hunting the aliens of 430-X for years and years. We've known about their plan to invade your planet for a long time. The problem was, we didn't know where they were going to set up their alien base, so it would be foolish for the Raeoleans to send warships to your planet without a specific location."

"You . . . you mean that the Raeoleans are going to come to Earth and battle the aliens from 430-X?" I asked.

"Exactly," Joey said with a nod. "You see, that's why I couldn't tell you I was an android. I didn't want anyone to know, for fear of the aliens from 430-X finding out about me."

"So that's why you knew so much about flying the spacecrafts," I said. "And how to program the navigational device that took us to 430-X."

"That's right," Joey replied. "While I hadn't piloted those particular brands of ships, most of them are similar in nature. If you're an experienced spacecraft pilot like me, it only takes a few minutes to catch on. Once you've commandeered one spacecraft, you've pretty much commandeered them all."

"So, while the other androids have been sent here by the aliens from 430-X, you've been sent here by the Raeoleans as a spy to find out where their alien base is?"

"Yes," Joey said. "You see, the aliens from 430-X are sort of like . . . well, they are like criminals. Bandits. They travel all through space, stealing valuable resources from planets such as Earth. If the aliens from 430-X succeed in stealing all of your water, what do you think would happen?"

A chill went down my spine, and I blinked. But I didn't have to say anything. Joey knew by the look on my face that I knew exactly what would happen.

He nodded knowingly. "That's right," he said. "The Raeoleans are sort of like an intergalactic police force, with a mission of stopping the criminal aliens."

"But why don't the Raeoleans just go to 430-X?" I asked. "Wouldn't that be easier?"

Joey shook his head. "No. You see, the aliens from 430-X—Xers, as Quantar called them—have thousands upon thousands of warships . . . many more than the

Raeoleans. The Raeoleans wait until the Xers travel to another planet, where only several dozen warships are needed. When the Xers invade, the Raeoleans can overtake them and destroy all of their ships. I've sent a homing signal off to the Raeolean command center, and they'll know exactly where to send their battleships."

"So there's going to be a battle?!?! Right here in the Grand Canyon?!?!" I exclaimed.

"Sooner than you think, I hope," Joey said with a nod. "Look out the window."

I snapped my head around suddenly . . . and gasped at what I saw in the sky.

37

Large spaceships, gleaming and shimmering in the sun, were descending into the canyon.

"The Raeoleans!" I exclaimed.

Joey shook his head. "Those are warships from 430-X," he said worriedly. "We can only hope that my signal reached the Raeolean command center in time."

"Isn't there anything we can do?" I asked.

"Yes," Joey replied. "We can wait. It's all we can do now."

Standing there, locked in that room, staring out the windows and watching the alien spaceships descend was *maddening*. I wished there was something we could do . . . and I hoped that the Raeolean spaceships would show up soon.

The spaceships from 430-X were landing all around us. Soon, I could see aliens wandering around. They looked, of course, just like the aliens we saw when we went to their planet.

Joey nervously scanned the sky.

"Something's wrong," he said. "The Raeoleans should have been here by now. Their ships are capable of traveling very, very fast . . . even faster than the aliens from 430-X."

I said nothing. I didn't want to think about what could happen if the Xers succeeded, but I couldn't help it. I tried to push the thoughts from my mind, but it just didn't work. I was so worried that I could hardly see straight.

After a while, I heard the roar of rockets starting up. Louder and louder, the warships readied from their base at the bottom of the Grand Canyon. Then I saw one rise up, then another. The building shook and the windows rattled. More and more alien craft took to the air.

"Where are they headed?" I asked.

"Several will head to the oceans," Joey replied. "More will remain right here in Arizona. They can access much of the world's water through a special process they've developed."

It was all very baffling. Many people have thought for years that there might be intelligent life on other planets, and I had concrete proof!

Stealing water from Earth really didn't seem all that intelligent, though.

"Well, we failed," Joey said despondently. "I really thought we could stop them, but I'm afraid—"

Joey was interrupted by an earthshattering explosion. I remember seeing one of the walls crashing in, and the roof above us coming down.

And then everything went dark.

38

Everything was dark.

I was really frightened, because I didn't know what had happened. But I wasn't hurt. There was debris all around and over me, and I struggled to push it away.

"Shelby!" I heard Joey shout. "Are you okay?"

"Yeah," I grunted, as I moved a piece of the wall away from me. "Are you?"

Joey laughed. "I'm an android," he said. "If I get broken, I can fix myself."

Gee . . . I hadn't thought of that. It was only a short while ago that I'd learned that Joey wasn't human.

"What happened?" I said as I pushed a portion of the ceiling off me. When I moved it away, sunlight streamed down upon me, and I could see again.

Joey didn't have to answer. High above us, a swarm of flying saucers were zipping across the sky. Laser blasts were shooting in every direction.

"The Raeoleans!" Joey shouted. *"They're here! They made it!"*

Sure enough, I could see the difference between the two spacecraft. The Xers were in spaceships that were oblong-shaped. Rocket thrusters jutted from the back, and laser cannons were mounted on the sides.

The Raeolean spaceships, however, were perfectly round and flat-looking, like a Frisbee. Lasers fired from ports on the sides of the craft.

"A stray laser shot probably hit the building we were in," Joey said. "Come on! We've got to take cover, just in case it happens again!"

"We can go over there!" I shouted, pointing at a large cave in the side of the canyon.

"Let's go!" Joey shouted, and we sprinted across the dusty canyon floor. Several androids scurried about, but they paid no attention to us. Either they thought that we were also androids, or they were too busy readying other spaceships for battle.

And when we reached the cave: jackpot!

Inside was a spacecraft, nearly identical to the one we had taken from the alien on 430-X! It was probably tucked away for safe keeping. There were no aliens or androids around it.

"Get in!" Joey shouted.

"Where are we going?!?!" I shouted back as the glass canopy raised. Joey leaped into the cockpit, and I quickly joined him in the passenger seat.

"For one, we're going to get away from the canyon. And we need to make sure that the androids don't carry out the alien's plans."

"What do you mean?" I asked as Joey fired up the spacecraft. We slowly raised up a few inches and Joey nudged the craft forward.

"If the aliens are defeated, the androids have been programmed to carry out their mission," Joey replied. "There are hundreds of androids in Arizona, and they will attempt to take over the world and gather up the water."

Great, I thought. *This gets worse with every passing minute.*

"But how are we going to stop them?" I asked. "If there are hundreds of androids in Arizona, how can we stop them all?"

"I've already thought about that," Joey said, "but I'm going to need your help."

The spaceship slowly left the cave and emerged in bright sunlight. High above, laser blasts streaked across the sky, and explosions could be seen and heard as the aliens battled. Joey guided the craft close to the canyon wall, and we rose up slowly.

"I want to stay out of sight for as long as possible," he explained. "Otherwise the Raeoleans may see our ship and fire at us, since we're in an alien craft."

When we were out of the canyon, Joey pushed the craft to full power, and we rocketed across the desert. The roar of the engines behind us was deafening.

"I need you to go to Mrs. Rodriguez's house," Joey shouted over the drone of the rockets.

"What?!?!" I exclaimed. "Why there?"

"I'm going to go back to 430-X. The androids are all programmed by a central computer system there. The programming signal is sent back to Earth, giving the androids their instructions. If I can somehow reprogram or destroy the computer, we can stop the androids from completing the mission, if the Raeoleans fail to destroy the Xers here on Earth."

"But why Mrs. Rodriguez's house?" I asked. "Why do I need to go there?"

Still piloting the craft, Joey dug into his pocket with his right hand and pulled out a quarter-sized object. He handed it to me. It was metallic, with little holes all over it.

"That's a space-time two-way radio," Joey explained. "We'll be able to talk to each other . . . even when I'm on 430-X. Since I'll be on their planet, I won't know if my plan to reprogram the androids succeeds. You'll be able to monitor Mrs. Rodriguez and let me know."

"But isn't Mrs. Rodriguez back there?" I asked, throwing my thumb over my shoulder. "In the Grand Canyon?"

"I think all of the androids have returned to their normal activities," Joey replied. "Their work is done, unless the aliens from 430-X are defeated by the Raeoleans. Then

176

they'll make preparations to follow through with the Xer's plans. I'll bet we'll find Mrs. Rodriguez's spacecraft hidden in the warehouse."

It was all very confusing, but Joey knew what he was talking about.

I hoped.

We arrived at the warehouse, and Joey guided the craft inside. Sure enough, Mrs. Rodriguez's spaceship was parked inside. We landed right next to it. The glass canopy opened and I got out, holding the tiny two-way radio he'd given me.

"How does this thing work?" I asked. There was no on/off switch, no buttons of any kind.

"It's solar powered," Joey said, "so it's always on. I'll radio you when I reach 430-X. You go to Mrs. Rodriguez's home and keep an eye on her. Stay out of sight, but keep an eye on her."

The glass canopy lowered, and Joey gave me the thumbs up sign from the cockpit. The craft rose up, traveled forward, and slipped out the open garage door. It rose up and out of sight, but I heard the roar of its engines as it departed.

I raced out of the warehouse and down the street, and I didn't stop until I rounded the corner of the block where Mrs. Rodriguez's home was. Then I casually slipped among the bushes near a house, following closely among the shrubbery until I reached Mrs. Rodriguez's house. Then I slipped behind the row of bushes in front of her home, determined to follow Joey's orders and watch to see what the android did.

And I didn't have long to wait.

39

I poked my head up slowly and peered through the living room window. Mrs. Rodriguez the android was in the kitchen with her back to me. She turned a little and I could see that she had put her human face back on. She was talking into her watch again, using that same, mechanical voice that I'd heard her use before. But I couldn't hear what she was saying.

When she turned once more, I ducked down. I certainly didn't want to get caught again!

The tiny two-way space-time radio was in my pocket, and I dug it out. It sure was amazing to think that the little metal device would allow me to talk to someone millions of miles away on another planet.

Mrs. Rodriguez's voice drew closer, and I knew that she had walked into the living room. Through the open window, I could hear what she was saying.

" . . . no, the Raeoleans showed up just as the invasion had started. I don't know how they were alerted to our location, but it appears that we have been defeated. I am awaiting orders to complete the mission with the others."

Joey was right! If the Xers fail—and it looked like they were going to—the androids were going to complete the mission!

Unless, of course, Joey's plan worked.

Mrs. Rodriguez's voice faded away. I was still hunkered down, but I figured that she probably had walked back into the kitchen.

Slowly, I rose up a little bit and peered through the window. I could see Mrs. Rodriguez talking into her watch . . . but I also saw something else.

A reflection in the window.

Someone was coming up behind me!

40

When I realized who it was and what they were doing, it was too late to try and run. A hand grasped my shoulder and spun me around. The tiny radio in my hand went flying. It vanished into the bushes.

It was Mr. Walinski, the school principal!

"Gotcha, you little troublemaker," he hissed, gripping my shoulder firmly. With his free hand, he opened the front door to Mrs. Rodriguez's house and pushed me inside. Mrs. Rodriguez spun when she heard the door open. She stopped talking into her watch and glared at me.

"You are becoming a problem, young lady," she said angrily.

At that point, I became angry myself. Oh sure, I was frightened, but I was also very mad. We had joked about Mr. Walinski being an android . . . and he really was!

"Me?!?!" I snapped back. "What you're doing is wrong! It's wrong . . . and you'll never get away with it!"

Mrs. Rodriguez laughed. Behind me, Mr. Walinski laughed, too.

"You may think that you've succeeded," Mr. Walinski said. "But you'll never stop us. We are androids, designed and programed by the aliens from 430-X, a superior race of beings. You humans are no match for us, no matter how many of you there are."

"It was silly of you to even try," Mrs. Rodriguez said.

"Well, we were able to signal the Raeoleans, weren't we?" I said smugly. "We stopped the alien invasion."

"You only succeeded in slowing down the inevitable," Mrs. Rodriguez said sharply. "You've done nothing to stop what we have set out to do."

I thought hard. I had to keep them talking as long as possible, because I had no idea how long it was going to take Joey to get back to 430-X and find the main programming computer.

"But why our planet?" I asked. "Why Earth?"

"Your planet holds a very large amount of water," Mr. Walinski replied. He adjusted his glasses, which I thought was kind of weird. Who ever heard of an android that wore glasses?

But then again, I've seen Mrs. Rodriguez wear glasses, and she's an android. Maybe it's only part of their disguise.

"There are many planets that have water," Mrs. Rodriguez said. "But none quite like Earth. Here, the water is much more accessible than it is on other planets."

182

"But why do they need so much water?" I asked, still stalling for time.

"Water is very important on 430-X," Mrs. Rodriguez continued. "On 430-X, water has many more uses than it does here on your planet. Water is used to create fuel. There, it can even be changed into a solid form without freezing it, therefore using it in many other ways. However, it takes massive amounts of water to do this . . . water that ran out on 430-X long ago."

"Sounds pretty irresponsible if you ask me," I said.

"I don't think you'll be needing to worry about irresponsibility," Mr. Walinski said with a chuckle. "It won't be long before Earth's water is compressed and shipped back to 430-X. Then our work here will be done."

"There are hundreds of androids at work, this very minute," Mrs Rodriguez said. "There is no way that you—"

She stopped speaking and made a short, jerky movement. Then another. She cocked her head to the side, and a strange look came over her face. Then she looked at me.

"Cookies," she said.

"Huh?" I replied.

"Cookies," she repeated. "I've made cookies. Would you like some?"

I was too confused to speak. One moment, she was telling me that all of Earth's water was about to be stolen by the Xers . . . now she was offering me cookies.

"I would *love* a cookie," Mr. Walinski said.

Mrs. Rodriguez turned and picked up a tray of cookies on the counter. "Chocolate chip," she said.

"My favorite," said Mr. Walinski as he took a cookie off the tray and popped it into his mouth.

Mrs. Rodriguez held out the tray to me. "Shelby?" was all she said.

I took a cookie. "Thank you," I said, "but I really have to get going. I've got homework to do."

"Well, you have a good evening," she said with a smile.

I turned and walked to the door. Neither android made any move to stop me.

It worked! Joey's plan really worked! He must've made it to 430-X and reprogrammed the androids from the main transmitting computer!

"See you in school," I said as I opened up the front door.

"Yes," Mr. Walinski replied. "See you in school."

I stepped out onto the porch and scanned the ground near the house. The tiny radio was in the grass, and I went over to it and picked it up.

"Joey?" I said as I held the small metal ball up to my lips. "Can you hear me? Joey?"

There was no answer. Maybe the thing had broken when I'd dropped it.

But there was one more problem that I faced, and it was a big one. I'd been gone a long time. No doubt Mom and Dad would be worried. Then they'd be furious.

I raced home, prepared for the worst.

41

As it turned out, it wasn't near as late as I thought it was. Mom and Dad weren't mad at all, but Mom wanted to know what I'd been doing all afternoon.

"Mom, you wouldn't believe it!" I said. "My teacher is an android! We took her spacecraft and went to a planet called 430-X and were captured by aliens! But we got away and came back to Earth and stopped the aliens from stealing all of our water!"

Mom was smiling. "All in one afternoon, huh?" she asked. "You must be hungry. I'll be sure to fill up your plate."

"Really, Mom! We were at the Grand Canyon when the Raeoleans arrived. They defeated the Xers! But Joey went back to 430-X and reprogrammed the computer that controls the androids! And guess what? Joey is an android, too!"

"That's nice, dear. Now . . . go wash up. Dinner will be ready in a little while."

I sighed, realizing that there was no way Mom or Dad were going to believe me.

We ate dinner, and I helped Mom with the dinner dishes. I tried to explain once again what had happened, but she just smiled and said that I should write it all down in a book. Nothing I could say would make her believe me.

"Look at that," I heard Dad say from the living room, where he was watching the TV news. "Some unidentified flying objects were reported over the Grand Canyon today," he said.

I raced into the living room. "See?!?!" I exclaimed. "I was there! I saw the spaceships!"

"Oh, don't be silly, Shelby," Dad said.

I gave up. There was no way that Mom and Dad were going to believe me.

I went into my bedroom and picked my notebook up off the dresser, then carried it to my bed. I decided to do what Mom had said: write down everything in a book. Maybe someday, someone would read it and believe me.

I wrote for a long time, until finally there was a gentle tapping on my door.

"Come in," I said.

The door opened, and Mom and Dad came in.

"We just wanted to show you something," Dad said. And with that, my parents reached up, placed their hands to their faces . . . and pulled away their masks.

Oh no! Even my Mom and Dad were androids

42

I was so freaked out that I could only gasp.

"That's right," Mom said as she came toward me. "We're androids, just like you."

Then I *did* scream. Mom was coming toward me, her arms extended like a zombie. Dad stood by the door, smiling.

"No!" I shrieked. "I'm not an android! I'm not an android!"

"Shelby," Mom said as she grasped my shoulders.

"No! Leave me alone! I don't want to be an android!"

"Shelby!" Mom shouted.

And that's when I opened my eyes . . . and woke up.

"What . . . what happened?" I asked groggily. Mom was kneeling by the bed, her hands on my shoulders. My heart was hammering in my chest.

"You were having a nightmare," she replied. "You must've fallen asleep while you were writing."

What a relief! I heaved a sigh. "Sorry about that," I said.

"It's getting late," she said. "Time for bed."

On Monday I was shocked to see Arielle in school. She came right up to me and started talking, acting perfectly normal!

"So . . . you don't remember what we did yesterday?" I asked her.

"Of course," she replied. "I worked on my homework all day."

Arielle had no memory of what we'd done at all!

Joey wasn't in class that day, but he showed up the following day. I talked with him in the lunchroom, and he remembered everything! He told me how he'd been able to reprogram the transmitting computer so that the androids on Earth would just continue to go about their business.

"But what about you?" I asked. "You're an android, too."

"Yes, and my work here is done. I'm not needed, but I am going to stay so I can keep an eye on the other androids. Just in case the Xers are able to regain control of them and try to use them to steal all of Earth's water."

But I had a lot of questions.

"Are your parents androids, too?" I asked.

Joey nodded. "Yes. They are called 'custodial androids.' They are programmed for different functions, but mainly, they make sure that my circuitry is working right."

"But if you're an android, why didn't you radio for help when our spaceship was out of control? Or when we'd been captured on 430-X?"

"A radio frequency might have blown my cover, and alerted the aliens from 430-X. Besides . . . I didn't have any way of actually communicating with the Raeoleans. The tiny radio I gave you was another item that I bargained from Quantar, in exchange for your plastic ring."

"Which reminds me," I said, digging into my pocket and pulling out the tiny, silver ball. "I think it's broken." I handed it back to Joey.

"Oh, it can be fixed easily enough," he said. "Don't worry about it."

We spent the rest of the lunch hour talking about what had happened. I told Joey that I was writing a story about it, but he suggested that I change everyone's names, just to be safe. He didn't want anyone at school to know that he was an android, and he didn't want anyone to know about Arielle, Mrs. Rodriguez, or Principal Walinski. After all, they weren't a danger to anyone anymore.

So that's what I did. I wrote down everything that happened. My book turned out to be over two hundred pages! I turned it in to Mrs. Rodriguez for extra credit, and she said that it was so good that she was going to enter it into a national contest!

And guess what? I won second place! It was really cool. They made an announcement over the school loudspeakers, and all of my classmates clapped. I felt really special.

But I wondered something.

Who won first place?

I didn't have to wait long for an answer. A few days later, I received my official notice in the mail. I'd won second place, and the notice also listed the names of a bunch of other winners. The first place winner was a kid named Chad Prescott from South Carolina. It listed a web address where his entire story was posted on-line, so the next day at the school's computer lab I logged on to read it.

And what a scary story it was! I don't know what was scarier . . . my experience with the androids and the aliens, or Chad's story. It was called

SOUTH CAROLINA SEA CREATURES
a true story
by Chad Prescott

And when I finished reading it, I was so scared that I vowed I would never, ever go swimming again . . . .

next in the

AMERICAN CHILLERS

SERIES:

#17:

SOUTH
CAROLINA
SEA
CREATURES

**turn the page to read a few
creepy chapters!**

1

Okay. The first thing you need to know about this story is that I'm not trying to scare you away from South Carolina. I've lived here my whole life, and my family vacations all over the state. We go camping at Lake Wateree, fishing at Lake Thurmond, and hiking at Hunters Island Nature Preserve.

And when it comes down to it, there really isn't anything to be afraid of. South Carolina has some alligators, which most states don't have. We also have a few poisonous snakes. Lots of states have those, and if you use a little common sense, the snakes won't bother you. There are sharks in the ocean, but I've never seen one, and I don't worry about them when I swim.

But what happened to me this past summer was different. It had nothing to do with snakes or alligators. True, what happened to me happened at the ocean, but it had nothing to do with sharks.

It had to do with sea creatures.

Hideous, ugly, gigantic creatures that no one had ever seen before.

But before I tell you about what happened *this* summer, it's important that you know something about what we went through *last* summer.

My name is Chad Prescott, and I live in Charleston, South Carolina. I'm twelve, and I have a sister named Michelle. She's ten, and while she can often be a real pain, most of the time she's pretty cool. She and I have the exact same color hair—brown—except hers is a lot longer than mine. She wears it in a ponytail a lot, especially when we're on vacation.

Which was where we were last summer when all of us—Mom, Dad, Michelle and me—had a horrifying experience.

We were staying at a place called Hilton Head Island. It's a famous place, and lots of people come here to golf, which is why we were at Hilton Head. Michelle and I don't golf, but Mom and Dad love the sport.

On this particular day, we had gone to the beach to swim in the ocean. The day was really warm, and the white beach sand was so hot that it stung my feet. Mom and Dad stayed on beach towels beneath a big blue and white umbrella, while Michelle and I went swimming . . . just like we always did when we spent a day at the beach.

And that's when something really scary happened.

2

I remember splashing around in the shallow water. We had met some new friends, but I don't remember their names.

What I do remember is what they were telling us about the Hilton Head Water Monster.

"He's big and green and he swallows people in one gulp," one of the kids was saying as we stood in the shallow water. The cool surf licked at my knees. Seagulls wheeled above, like white kites beneath a blue sky.

"There's no such thing," I said, shaking my head. But Michelle was falling for it.

"Really?" she asked.

"Yep," another kid said, nodding. "It's true. I've seen it before."

I shook my head. "I don't believe you," I said.

"Believe what you want," the kid replied. "I'm telling you: ask around. Lots of people have seen the monster. He waits until you're not paying attention. You might be swimming, even in shallow water. You won't see the monster until it's too late."

"And then what?" Michelle asked. Her blue eyes were bulging like marbles.

"And then it grabs you," the kid said, "and pulls you under. One gulp, and you're gone."

Michelle looked positively horrified, and I didn't think it was very nice of the kids to be scaring her that way.

But they kept going. I think they saw how frightened Michelle was, and knew that she believed their story.

After they left, Michelle stared out at the waves rolling in. She looked worried.

"They were only trying to scare you," I told her. "There's no such thing as the Hilton Head Water Monster."

"But what if there is?" she replied.

"There just *isn't*," I said.

"But how do you know, Chad? It could be out there right now, just waiting."

"Look out there," I said. "Lots of people are swimming and having fun. Do you think they're worried about some silly water monster?"

"Maybe they don't know about it," she said.

"For gosh sakes," I said, wading into deeper water. "Come on." I turned and reached out my hand. Reluctantly, Michelle took it.

"Those kids were just being mean," I said. "There's nothing out here. You'll see."

Soon, the water was up over our waists. A wave washed up and almost knocked us over, and Michelle spluttered and giggled.

"See?" I said, with my best *big-brother-knows-best* voice. "Nothing to worry about at all."

As soon as I uttered those words, a dark shape appeared in the water before us. It was big and wide, but the form was too dark to make out what it was. But I knew one thing:

It was moving *fast*.

Michelle screamed, but it was already too late. The enormous beast was already upon us.

3

I think that if I had the time, I would have screamed, too. But the creature was moving too fast, and in the next instant I was knocked beneath the surface. Salt water filled my mouth, burned my nostrils, and stung my eyes.

But I still had Michelle's hand, and I wasn't going to let go. I held tight with all my strength as bubbles whirled about. My foot found the soft, sandy bottom and I broke the surface. I pulled Michelle to her feet. She was coughing and choking, and then she started to cry. My head snapped around, searching the water, ready to face the awful creature that was after us.

But it was gone.

"Come on," I said, leading my sister to shallow water. "Let's get out and go tell Mom and Dad."

All around us, there were people splashing and having fun. No one else had spotted the gigantic creature . . . yet.

But I knew it was only a matter of time.

We couldn't get out of the water fast enough. When the waves were beneath our knees, we started to run. Michelle had stopped crying, but I knew that she was still scared, so I didn't let go of her hand.

When we reached the shore, we ran across the hot sand to where Mom and Dad were sitting.

"Mom! Dad!" I exclaimed. "There's something in the water!"

"A monster!" Michelle said. She turned and pointed out to sea. "It was after us! It really was!"

Mom and Dad looked concerned. They stood up and raised their hands to their foreheads to shield their eyes from the harsh midday sun.

"Right out there," I said, pointing.

"It's the Hilton Head Water Monster," Michelle said. "We met some kids that told us that the Hilton Head Water Monster can swallow you up in one gulp!"

Dad lowered his hand and looked at Michelle. "There is no such thing as the Hilton Head Water Monster," he said. "They were only trying to fool you."

"But there's something out there," Michelle protested.

"Michelle's right," I said. "Something big knocked us over."

"It was probably just a wave," Mom said. She sat down on her beach towel.

"I'm going to go to the snack bar," Dad said. "Anybody want anything?"

I was about to tell him that I wanted some lemonade, but the words never left my lips. I was interrupted by a loud commotion in the water.

Screaming.

Shouting.

The day was hot, but a cold chill raced down my spine as I realized that there was something in the sea, after all. Michelle and I had been lucky. We had escaped.

But as we stood watching the disturbance, I knew that other people weren't going to be so fortunate.

FUN FACTS ABOUT ARIZONA:

State Capitol: Phoenix

State Fossil: Petrified Wood

State Nickname: The Grand Canyon State

State Gemstone: Turquoise

State Bird: Cactus Wren

State Motto: "Ditat Deus" (God enriches)

State Tree: Palo Verde

State Mammal: Ringtail

State Flower: Saguaro Cactus

Statehood: February 14th, 1912 (48th state)

FAMOUS ARIZONA PEOPLE!

Geronimo, Apache Indian chief

Barry Goldwater, politician

Linda Ronstadt, singer

Kerri Strug, gymnast

Lynda Carter, actress

Rex Allen, singer, actor

Cochise, Apache Indian chief

Cesar Estrada Chavez, labor leader

Frank Luke, JR, WW1 fighting ace

among many, many more!

Also by Johnathan Rand:

GHOST IN THE GRAVEYARD